FOUR
HOBOKEN
STORIES

DANIEL PINKWATER

DOVER PUBLICATIONS, INC.
MINEOLA, NEW YORK

FOUR
HOBOKEN
STORIES

Contents

Introduction

In the days of my comparative youth I resided in a small
apartment, which I shared with a number of rats, on the
east side of Manhattan. It was my intention to be some
kind of artist; a painter or a sculptor. I had big ideas, and
as I mentioned, the apartment was small. It was also dark,
was up several flights of stairs, and the sound of the rats
scurrying inside the walls was hard to get used to.

*What I need is a studio, a great big space with plenty of
light*, I thought. Artists in New York, in those days, and I
suppose today, would occupy lofts—industrial spaces in
old buildings. These were highly prized and hard to come
by. Something many of the artists in New York had in common was David Davis Fine Art Supplies. It was a shop in
one of those lofts, where you could buy paints and can-
vas, paper, brushes, and also get advice from David Davis
himself. David Davis was a little man with a beard and a
bald head—he looked exactly like the famous painter
Cézanne. David Davis knew everything. Great and famous
artists were his customers, and he helped them in so
many ways.

Here's an example: No less a great and famous artist
than Salvador Dalí gave David Davis some watercolors to
mount and frame for him. David Davis put his coffee cup
on one of the paintings and it made a brown ring. I forgot

to mention that David Davis was a complete slob. He was upset. He phoned Dalí.

"Maître, I made a coffee ring on one of your pictures," he confessed.

"Mount it anyway!" Dali said. "People will think I did it on purpose."

"David, I need a loft," I told David Davis.

"I have one for you, but you have to like music," he said. David Davis often said things no one understood. He told me to take the ferryboat to Hoboken, and see the Judge.

"There's a ferryboat that goes to Hoboken? Where and what is Hoboken? Who is the Judge?"

The ride across the Hudson River was very nice, and the Judge, who was the town magistrate, and who owned the building the loft was in, was very nice, and the loft was big and beautiful, and cheap. I rented it, and the Judge came over with cans of paint. The loft was a hideous pink at the time—I painted it white. It took a week.

Then I moved in. I found out why David Davis had said I'd have to like music. The bar downstairs had a very loud band on weekends. It was a lousy band, but I didn't mind. I loved my loft, and it turned out I loved Hoboken. I lived there for 12 years.

–Daniel Pinkwater
2017

THE MAGIC MOSCOW

This is a somewhat true story. My friend Steve, who was in actual fact the biggest baby ever born in Budapest, ran an ice cream and hamburger joint very much like the one in the story. The rest I made up. Now this is interesting in a literary way: It is part of a trilogy. A trilogy, as you probably know, is a group of three books that go together. Either they are sequels and continue a story, or have the same characters, or are set in the same place, or for some reason or other the author thinks they're related. The second part of this trilogy is Attila the Pun, *included in this book. There is a third part,* Slaves of Spiegel, *which wasn't available for publication in this volume, but you can find it elsewhere. Also interesting in a literary way is the fact that* Slaves of Spiegel, *while part of what let's call The Magic Moscow Trilogy, is also a sequel to another book we don't have in this collection,* Fat Men from Space. *I don't know why I do things like this.*

1

Everybody knows what a Magic Moocow is. They're everywhere. They're those soft ice cream stands—the ones with the big plaster sculpture of a cow's head on top. There used to be a Magic Moocow in Hoboken, but it was taken over by my friend Steve Nickelson. He changed it into the Magic Moscow, by painting out the second "o" in Moocow and painting in an "s." He also painted the cow's head with diagonal purple and orange stripes.

Steve Nickelson is my friend. He's also my boss. I have a part-time job at the Magic Moscow. In the summer, I work full-time.

It's interesting working for Steve. He's a big guy with a bushy brown beard. He always wears a white shirt with the tail hanging out. On the tail is a black stamp that says "Bandini's Linen Service—Union City, N.J." He wears white pants from Bandini's, too. He never wears anything else—even when he's not working—even when he's wandering around the streets of Hoboken.

Steve is a collector. He collects any number of things. He collects comic books: he has almost a half-million of them. He collects old records. He has a lot of them, too. He collects old pennies. He collects bottlecaps. He collects antique sneakers and basketball shoes. Once he started a collection of twigs and small sticks. He put advertisements in newspapers all over the country, and people sent him twigs and small sticks. Another collection he started was beans. He tried to get one of every kind of bean on earth.

Steve tends to get tired of the little collections, like antique sneakers, twigs, and beans. The ones he really works on are the comics, old records, science-fiction books, and old magazines.

My part-time job is helping Steve in the Magic Moscow, but sometimes I help him with his collections. Sometimes, I just sit around in the Magic Moscow, after closing time, looking through comics with Steve and listening to old records. He keeps a lot of his collections in the back of the store.

This particular summer, Steve went on a Sergeant Schwartz of the Yukon kick. Sergeant Schwartz of the Yukon is a Canadian mountie. He always gets his man. And he has this smart dog. The dog's name is Hercules. That's the name of the television program, "Sergeant Schwartz of the Yukon and His Great Dog Hercules." It's an old program. It isn't on regular TV anymore. Steve got in the habit of leaving work at three-thirty every day to watch reruns on UHF. He also started collecting *Sergeant Schwartz of the Yukon and His Great Dog Hercules* comic books. He read them all the time. Once he found a Sergeant Schwartz record. He also got some posters—old ones—and his dearest wish was to see one of the *Sergeant Schwartz of the Yukon and His Great Dog Hercules* movies that they made years ago.

All the time, Steve used to whistle the theme song from "Sergeant Schwartz of the Yukon and His Great Dog Hercules."

He really loved Sergeant Schwartz of the Yukon—and he really loved the great dog Hercules.

After a while, it appeared to me that Steve loved the great dog Hercules even more than Sergeant Schwartz. Every time a big dog, like a German shepherd, went by the Magic Moscow Steve would watch it until it was out of sight. Sometimes, when he was cleaning out the giant soft-ice-cream machines, I would hear Steve having an imaginary conversation: "Get up, you huskies—Get up, Hercules," he would say under his breath. And he'd make barking and woofing noises, too.

It was only a matter of time.

In the back of an old copy of *Sergeant Schwartz of the Yukon and His Great Dog Hercules: Comics and Stories*, Steve found an advertisement:

Boys and girls! You can have a real
ALASKAN MALAMUTE
Just like Sergeant Schwartz's great dog
HERCULES!!!!!!!!
Gold Rush Kennels, Nutley, New Jersey

It was an old magazine, but the Gold Rush Kennels were still there: Steve made sure by telephoning. Then he started locking up the Magic Moscow. "Come on, Norman," he said to me, "we're going to look at some dogs!"

2

We piled into Steve's little car and took off. About an hour later, we pulled up in front of the Gold Rush Kennels in Nutley, New Jersey. It was just an ordinary house. The only thing that told us it was a kennel was the sign in front.

We rang the bell. A big fat guy in his undershirt came to the door. He was smoking a cigarette, and he needed a shave.

"How do you do," the big fat guy said. "I am John Crisco, the proprietor of Gold Rush Kennels. Are you the gentleman who called?"

"I'm Steve Nickelson," Steve said, "and this is my friend, Norman Bleistift."

John Crisco smelled of after-shave or deodorant. He had oily stuff in his hair. "And how may I help you?" he asked.

"Well, we thought we'd like to look at your dogs, if that's all right with you," Steve said.

"Look?" John Crisco said. "Of course you can look. That's no problem. You can look, sure. Look all you want. But I hope you aren't planning to buy a puppy. My puppies are not for sale to just anybody. Only very special people can buy my puppies. I have to know a lot about you before you take a puppy away from here. So you can look, but don't think I'm going to sell you a puppy."

6

John Crisco took us by the hands and led us out the back door.

In the yard, there were dogs in rows of cages. When they saw us, they went wild. They barked and wagged their tails, and they stood up with their front feet on the wire doors of their cages.

The place was dirty. It smelled.

"Please pardon the appearance of this place," John Crisco said. "The boy who cleans up got sick today, and I haven't had a chance to tidy up."

Steve didn't hear him. All the dogs looked more or less like Sergeant Schwartz's great dog Hercules, and Steve was fascinated.

Steve walked up and down in front of the cages. Sometimes he would stop and look at a puppy. "Ooooh, I like this one," he would say, or "This one is cute." The puppies were going crazy. I guess they were hoping that Steve would take them out of those dirty cages and give them a home.

"I can see you know a lot about dogs," John Crisco said. "The puppies you seem to like are the very best ones. Some of them are almost as good as Platinum Blazing Yukon Flash."

"Platinum Blazing Yukon Flash?" Steve asked.

"Yes, the finest puppy I've seen in many a year," John Crisco said. "His grandfather was the dog who played Sergeant Schwartz's dog, Hercules, on television—you know, Sergeant Schwartz of the Yukon. The grandfather's name was Champion Goldentooth Gorilla."

"Gosh," Steve said, "Sergeant Schwartz's dog's grandson! Is he here? Could we see him?"

"Aha!" John Crisco shouted. "I knew it all along! You want to get me to sell him to you. You didn't fool me by pretending you had never heard of him! Shame on you, trying to trick me like that!"

"Mr. Crisco, I'm not trying to trick you," Steve said. "I'd just like to have a look at him. Is he really the grandson of the great dog Hercules, I mean, Champion Goldentooth Gorilla?"

"I'll never let him go!" John Crisco shouted. "It doesn't matter that I'm poor and have all these other dogs to feed and take care of. I will keep Platinum Blazing Yukon Flash—somehow. Somehow, I will find a way to keep him and take him to dog shows, so he can win ribbons and become a famous champion. I don't know how I'll manage it, but I'll do it!" John Crisco was crying. He threw his big fat body to the ground, made little moaning noises, and beat on the ground with his fists and feet.

"There, there, Mr. Crisco," Steve said, "I didn't mean to upset you." John Crisco paid no attention: he continued to moan and drum on the ground. "We'll just be going now," Steve said. "We only wanted to have a look." Steve started to move away from John Crisco.

"Look? Of course you may look." John Crisco sprang to his feet. It was surprising to see such a fat man move so quickly. "Just remember, he's not for sale."

John Crisco took a padlock off the door to his garage. "I don't keep him in with the ordinary dogs," he said.

It was dark in the garage. Out of the shadows came a funny-looking puppy, blinking in the sunlight. I put out my hand, and he licked it. He smelled of the same after-shave that John Crisco used. Someone had brushed him recently—I could tell, because his hair was parted in the middle, just like John Crisco's.

"That's Platinum Blazing Yukon Flash?" Steve asked.

"Well, I just call him Edward for short," John Crisco said.

"But he looks kind of scrawny and sickly," Steve said. "His head is too big and his feet are floppy and he's coughing."

John Crisco slapped Steve on the back. "Now, don't tease. We real dog fanciers should be honest with one another. I was watching you in the kennels, and I can see that you know a good dog when you see one. Either you're an expert—or, even better, a natural genius when it comes to dogs. Now, tell me, doesn't he look exactly like his grandfather, Champion Goldentooth Gorilla?"

Steve squinted and put his head sideways, looking at the puppy, who was now sitting down and blinking—once he sneezed. "Isn't he kind of small?" Steve asked.

"He's big for his size," John Crisco said. "Just feel him."

John Crisco lifted the puppy and handed him to Steve. The puppy licked his face. "I guess I see what you mean. I guess he is sort of big for his size."

"This is the greatest puppy I've ever raised," John Crisco said. "When he grows up, he'll be a famous Alaskan Malamute and win ribbons and trophies and be a great champion. All my life I've hoped to someday have a dog as good as this one will be. I'll tell you something about this dog, I've decided to give him to you."

"What?" Steve shouted. "You want to give him to me? Your best dog ever? Platinum Blazing Yukon Flash?"

"Yes," John Crisco said, "he belongs with someone who can really take care of him and give him every advantage. I know you will take Edward—I call him Edward for short, you know—to lots of dog shows and help him to become a famous champion."

John Crisco was crying again. The puppy had jumped into Steve's arms and was licking his face, and John Crisco was hugging them both.

"But I can't just take him away," Steve said. "I can't just accept the best puppy you ever had as a gift."

"Well, if it will make you feel any better about it," John Crisco said, "you can give me three hundred dollars for him."

John Crisco counted the money three times, before we loaded Edward, also known as Platinum Blazing Yukon Flash, into Steve's little car.

As we drove away, John Crisco waved to us and kissed the bundle of bills from time to time.

3

Even though Steve is technically an adult, he still lives with his mother and father. When he introduced Edward to them, they told him that Edward was not invited to live in their house. You really couldn't blame them. Large portions of Steve's comic book, record, and sneaker collections—those things that wouldn't fit in the back room of the Magic Moscow—were already in the house and his mother and father hardly had room to move around.

So we tried taking Edward to live at my house. My parents were very unfair. They just said no, without any really good reason, except that they're both allergic to dogs.

So Edward went to live in the Magic Moscow.

The after-shave lotion that John Crisco had squirted him with was beginning to wear off, and Edward smelled pretty stale. We gave him three baths, which helped a little. After his baths, Edward crawled under a table and went to sleep.

"Are you sure that he's going to be a famous show dog?" I asked.

"Of course he is," Steve said. "He looks just like his grandfather, Champion Goldentooth Gorilla. Didn't you see how John Crisco hated to part with him? When he grows up, he will be a famous dog and win lots of ribbons."

Edward coughed in his sleep under the table.

"Then why didn't John Crisco keep him?" I asked. We looked at Edward. His head was too big for his body, and his feet were floppy. When he walked around, he kept bumping into things.

We took Edward to the vet, who gave him some medicine for his cough. The vet said he was not a very healthy puppy, but if we took extra good care of him and fed him well, he might grow up to be big and strong.

Edward liked living in the Magic Moscow. He liked Steve and me. He liked getting all the food and water he wanted. Every night Steve would make him a grilled cheese sandwich, as a special treat, before we went home. Edward's cough got better.

We expected him to get bigger, but we weren't prepared for how fast he got bigger and how big he got. He got to be *very* big *very* fast. His head got bigger, too; but he still kept tripping and bumping into things because his feet were still too big for his body.

Edward liked the people who came to the Magic Moscow. When someone he especially liked came, he would jump up and down, trip and fall down, and lick their faces. At other times, he would lie behind the counter asleep, snoring and growling. Even after months of baths, he still had a faint smell like very old basketball shoes.

For a long time, Edward was afraid of trucks. Whenever one went past, he would shriek and jump in the air.

Edward got over being afraid of trucks. Then he took up singing. He usually sang at night, and the people who lived near the Magic Moscow would call Steve on the telephone and make suggestions about Edward.

For a long time, Edward went through a period of liking to fight with other dogs. Whenever Edward saw another dog, he would try to chomp it. He especially wanted to fight big dogs, and Steve or I would have to drag him away, snarling and growling. Steve thought that maybe Edward had had a bad experience when he was little.

Steve didn't know how right he was. One day a customer came to the Magic Moscow. His name was Davis Davis, and he was a world-famous dog expert. He told us so.

"That looks like one of John Crisco's Malamutes," Davis Davis said.

"That's right," Steve said. "Can you tell just by looking?"

"Friend, there's very little I don't know about dogs," Davis Davis said, "and I know quite a bit about the famous Mr. John Crisco, too."

"Such as what?" Steve asked.

"Well, for one thing, he doesn't feed his dogs enough. He doesn't give them enough water either, which is even meaner. And he doesn't take them to the vet. If they get sick, they just get better on their own—or else."

"Or else?" Steve asked.

"Or else." Davis Davis continued, "John Crisco is mean to all his dogs but one. That is the only really good dog he has—at least he thinks so. See, he has this gigantic Malamute named Prince Razorback of Mukamuk. He must weigh two hundred pounds. He's the biggest Malamute that ever lived—also the meanest. He lives in John Crisco's own house, mostly under the kitchen sink, thinking evil thoughts. He sleeps in John Crisco's own bed. John Crisco feeds him Hershey bars, which is the only reason he has never bitten John Crisco. That dog loves Hershey bars. Say, could I have one of those Moron's Delights?"

The Moron's Delight is one of Steve's specialties. It has six flavors of ice cream—two scoops of each—a banana, a carrot, three kinds of syrup, whole roasted peanuts, a slice of Swiss cheese, a radish, yogurt, wheat germ, and a kosher pickle. It is served in a shoebox lined with plastic wrap. Steve considers it a health-food dessert.

While Steve was making the Moron's Delight, Davis Davis went on about John Crisco: "At night, John Crisco lets Prince Razorback of Mukamuk go out to the kennels and terrify the dogs and puppies, poor things. If Prince

Razorback of Mukamuk sees a nose or a paw sticking out of a cage, he just chomps it. He's a nasty dog.

"Every now and then, John Crisco takes Prince Razorback to a dog show," Davis Davis went on. "He touches him up with a fountain pen, squirts a lot of aftershave lotion on him, and takes him out to win a blue ribbon. Of course he usually scares the judges so badly that he wins. But the really interesting thing about John Crisco is the way he can sell dogs. He makes up all sorts of high-sounding names for them and gets people to pay six times what the dog is worth. One of his favorite tricks is telling people that a dog is the grandson of Sergeant Schwartz's dog, Hercules. Well, first of all, Hercules was never a Malamute in the first place: he was a Saint Bernard with a lot of makeup. Also, he never did have any puppies. Yes, sir, that John Crisco is quite an operator."

Davis Davis walked away, eating his Moron's Delight with a plastic spoon as he went.

"Do you think he's right?" I asked Steve. "Do you think that John Crisco is a swindler?"

"No," Steve said. "That Davis Davis doesn't know everything."

Then he looked at Edward for a long time.

"You know," Steve said, "even if Edward doesn't become a famous champion and win prizes at dog shows, he's a very nice dog, just the same."

"I think so, too," I said.

That night Steve put a scoop of ice cream on top of Edward's grilled cheese sandwich.

4

Naturally, we use a lot of milk at the Magic Moscow. The guy who sells us the milk is a friend of Steve's. His name is Bruce, and he's an interesting person. The most interesting thing about Bruce is Cheryl, his horse. Bruce says she's the last horse in Hoboken. Bruce brings the milk in a horse-drawn milk wagon. Cheryl pulls it, of course. Cheryl is the only horse I know. She's a real old horse. She's white with pink around her wrinkled old nose and watery brown eyes.

Bruce is always talking about what a smart horse Cheryl is. I never saw her do anything to show that she's smart. I mean, she's a nice horse, and I always used to go outside when Bruce delivered the milk and feed Cheryl some stale bread—and she'd sort of snort and nuzzle me—but that doesn't go to show any special intelligence.

Usually when Bruce would come by with the milk, he'd sit around in the Magic Moscow, having a bowl of soup and telling Steve how smart his horse was. He said that Cheryl had correctly predicted the outcome of the last five presidential elections. I never heard her say a word.

When Edward came to live at the Magic Moscow, the conversations between Steve and Bruce changed. Bruce would still brag about how smart his horse was, but now Steve had an animal to brag about. He'd tell Bruce how smart Edward was. He'd also talk about Edward's famous grandfather, Champion Goldentooth Gorilla, the dog who played Sergeant Schwartz of the Yukon's dog on television.

Meanwhile, Edward fell in love with Cheryl. He thought she was the most wonderful thing he'd ever seen. The first time Bruce and Cheryl came by, after we'd just brought Edward to the Magic Moscow, Edward went crazy. He whined and barked and jumped up and down at the window.

We took Edward outside and introduced him to the horse. He licked Cheryl's nose, and she nuzzled him and made little grunting noises.

After that, Cheryl would whinny for Edward. Edward would bark and whine and howl until we let him out. Then he'd cavort on the sidewalk, giving Cheryl kisses on the nose, and Cheryl would reach down and bump Edward lovingly.

Sometimes we'd let Edward go off with Bruce and Cheryl. He'd ride in the milk wagon, smiling and wagging his tail and barking.

Not far from the Magic Moscow is a park where Steve and I would take Edward for exercise. One day there was a sign posted in the park saying that the Hoboken Sled Dog Club was going to have its annual show in that very park on the following Saturday. We decided we'd enter Edward—just for fun.

We didn't know it, but early in the morning on that following Saturday, John Crisco got up extra early. He fed all the dogs at Gold Rush Kennels in Nutley, New Jersey, and then he coaxed Prince Razorback out from under the sink by offering him Hershey bars.

John Crisco put an extra lot of oily stuff on his hair and squirted himself and Prince Razorback of Mukamuk all over with aftershave lotion. John Crisco also put on his special lucky shirt he had brought back from Florida and touched up Prince Razorback's fur here and there with a fountain pen.

John Crisco coaxed Prince Razorback of Mukamuk into the back seat of his car, again by offering him Hershey bars. Then, wearing his special lucky shirt, his sunglasses, and his white tennis shoes, John Crisco started out for the Hoboken Sled Dog Club's annual show.

When Steve and I arrived with Edward, the park was already full of Malamutes. There were big ones and small ones, tall ones and short ones, black and white ones, gray ones, red ones, brown ones, tough ones, silly ones. There were dozens and dozens of Malamutes, with pink tongues flapping, tails wagging, barking and howling, growling and whining, and squeaking and mumbling.

Malamutes like other Malamutes better than anything. They like to play with each other, show off for each other, and pick fights with each other. Edward had never seen so many Malamutes since his days at Gold Rush Kennels of Nutley, New Jersey.

He just stood there for a while, figuring it out. Then he began to wag his tail.

"I don't think he sees anybody that he wants to fight with," I said.

"I'm sure Edward will behave," Steve said. "I'll go and enter him in the dog show now."

"I'm going to walk around," I said. "I'll catch up with you later."

There were rings, like boxing rings, set up for the dogs to be shown in. There was a table with silver cups and little statues, the prizes that would go to the winners. Next to that was a table where people, wearing ribbons that said OFFICIAL," were writing down the names of the dogs that were entered in the show. Steve told them to write down Platinum Blazing Yukon Flash, and they gave him a cardboard number to wear on his arm.

"Go to ring number three, and wait for your number to be called," one of the officials told Steve.

John Crisco arrived with Prince Razorback of Mukamuk. He had a hard time persuading Prince Razorback to get out of the car. After eating six Hershey bars, Prince Razorback finally decided to get out and go with John Crisco to the tables where the officials were taking down names. All the way from the car to the official's table, Prince Razorback made a low growling noise in his throat and looked from side to side as people and dogs got out of his way.

"Go to ring number three and wait for your number to be called," the official told John Crisco. John Crisco and Prince Razorback went to ring number three, where Steve and Edward were waiting. John Crisco had forgotten Steve and Edward, and Steve was waving to me on the other side of the ring, so he didn't see John Crisco. But apparently Edward remembered John Crisco—and he especially remembered Prince Razorback of Mukamuk. Edward also remembered that he was a big dog now. And he remembered all the practice he'd had trying to chomp dogs around Hoboken.

Edward lunged forward, pulling his leash out of Steve's hand. He ran at Prince Razorback and chomped him on the nose—hard. Prince Razorback had never been chomped in all his life. He was so big that dogs had always been afraid of him. He had done all the chomping. Prince Razorback wasn't exactly scared, but he was so surprised that he did a backward somersault and started running. Edward ran after him, growling and screaming.

When Prince Razorback started to run he broke the heavy chain that was attached to his collar, and John Crisco fell over backward, on top of Steve who was just turning around to see what had happened.

John Crisco and Steve struggled to their feet and began running after their dogs, shouting to them to come back.

Edward chased Prince Razorback all around the park. When some of the dogs saw Prince Razorback running straight at them, they got scared, broke away, and started running from him. Some of the other dogs saw Prince Razorback and Edward run past them, and broke away and started running after them. The dogs' owners ran after them, shouting to them to come back.

There were soon one hundred and twenty-two dogs, including Prince Razorback and Edward, running as fast as they could around the park: sixty dogs running away from Prince Razorback, sixty-one dogs, including Edward, running after him. And there were one hundred and twenty-two owners, including John Crisco and Steve, running after them.

Prince Razorback was not very bright. He didn't have many ideas, but as he was running, he started to have one: "Why Prince Razorback run from all stupid little dogs?" he thought. "Better Prince Razorback chase *them*." Prince Razorback of Mukamuk stopped and turned around. He made an awful face and ran at the dogs who had been running after him. All the dogs screamed and started running the other way—all except Edward, who stood still and got ready to fight. But Prince Razorback had forgotten all about Edward's chomping him on the nose. He was interested in chasing the sixty-one dogs who had been chasing him. He crashed right into Edward and ran over him.

When the one hundred and twenty-two owners saw half the dogs running toward them, they started waving their arms and shouting, "Here, girl!" "Come, boy!" They tried to catch their dogs, but the dogs slipped past them.

The dogs who had not been running after Prince Razorback stopped when they noticed that no one was chasing them anymore. Then they saw all the dogs running in the opposite direction—away from Prince Razorback—and started running after them. They ran right over Edward, who was just getting over being knocked down by Prince Razorback.

There was a little lake in the park, and Prince Razorback chased the dogs who were running away from him right into it. Then he jumped in after them. Once they were in the water, the dogs forgot about chasing and being chased. Even Prince Razorback calmed down and floated on his back, waving his paws in the air.

All the owners lined up on the edge of the little lake and shouted to their dogs to come back. Then the other bunch of dogs, the ones who had been running away from Prince Razorback and then turned around, arrived at the edge of the lake, going fast. They bumped into the crowd of owners and knocked most of them into the water. Then the dogs jumped in, too.

I found Edward, walking in circles, shaking his head to get over being knocked down twice and run over by one hundred and twenty-one Malamutes. Steve came along, dripping, and picked up Edward's leash and led him back to ring number three, where the judge was waiting.

In the lake the owners were splashing around, trying to catch their dogs and drag them up the muddy, slippery bank.

Edward won a blue ribbon—also a red ribbon, a yellow ribbon, and a white ribbon. He won six silver cups, too, because every other dog was soaking wet, covered with mud, or still swimming in the lake.

It was late afternoon when we took Edward back to the Magic Moscow, along with the blue, red, yellow, and white ribbons and the six silver cups.

Most of the other dogs had been caught and taken home. Some of the owners were drying off their dogs with towels. John Crisco was tired after all the running and swimming, and he and Prince Razorback were floating on their backs, eating some Hershey bars that John Crisco had in his pockets.

"I think Edward did very well for his first time," Steve said.

"Me, too," I said. "I'm sure he would have won even if all the other dogs hadn't jumped in the lake."

Steve arranged all of Edward's trophies and ribbons over the counter at the Magic Moscow. He made Edward a Moron's Delight to celebrate his winning.

When customers came to the Magic Moscow, they asked Steve, "Did your dog win all those ribbons and trophies?"

"Of course he did," Steve said. "He's a very important dog. He is the grandson of Champion Goldentooth Gorilla, the dog that played Hercules, Sergeant Schwartz of the Yukon's dog. His name is Platinum Blazing Yukon Flash, but we just call him Edward."

5

After a while, things began to quiet down. Steve had bragged to everybody in town, and Edward had wandered off to nap in the alley behind the Magic Moscow. Steve spent a lot of time looking at the trophies and ribbons. He was really happy.

Bruce the milkman came by, without Cheryl, and Steve told him how Edward had beaten four hundred Malamutes at the dog show. Every time he told the story, he'd add a few dogs to the number to make the competition seem stiffer.

Bruce the milkman was a little jealous, I could tell. Even though he claimed Cheryl was the smartest horse in the world, it would be too farfetched to claim that she had ever been in, much less won, a horse show. Still, he tried to be a good sport, and he congratulated Steve.

While Steve and Bruce the milkman were talking, a stranger came into the Magic Moscow. He was tall and neat looking, with one of those thin mustaches. He had high boots on and a sort of cowboy hat.

When Steve saw the stranger, his mouth dropped open, and his eyes opened wide.

"Excuse me," said the stranger, "I'm trying to find the park. There's supposed to be a dog show today, and I'm afraid I've missed it. The traffic on the New Jersey Turnpike was just awful."

Steve was trying to talk. He couldn't seem to get any words to come out. He just went, "Uh . . . uh . . . uh . . . uh."

Finally Steve managed to get himself together. "It's Sergeant Schwartz!" he shouted. "It's Sergeant Schwartz of the Yukon! Right here! In my store!" Then he fainted.

He didn't actually faint all the way, out cold on the floor. He just staggered and had to grab the counter for support.

"Are you all right, old man?" Sergeant Schwartz asked and patted Steve on the shoulder.

"He patted me on the shoulder!" Steve shouted. "He called me old man!" Then he fainted again.

Bruce the milkman explained, "He's a big fan of yours."

"I didn't know I had any fans left," Sergeant Schwartz said. "I haven't worked in years."

Sergeant Schwartz of the Yukon and Bruce the milkman led Steve to a chair and lowered him into it. He was muttering, "Right here in my store—Sergeant Schwartz of the Yukon—right here—it's too much—too much."

Sergeant Schwartz's real name was Pierre Beeswax. He was an actor who played the famous mountie on television; but there was no explaining that to Steve, who insisted he was nobody other than his hero Sergeant Schwartz.

Outside the Magic Moscow there was a really gaudy panel truck. It was bright red and really shiny, with gold trim and a picture of an Alaskan Malamute. In gold letters on the side of the truck were the words

HERCULES, GREAT DOG OF THE NORTH.

"Mr. Beeswax," I said, "is Hercules out there in the truck?"

Steve was just coming out of his trance. "Hercules? Is he here, too? The great lead dog of the north? Oooh, Sergeant Schwartz, let us see him. I love Hercules. I've got all the comic books, and I've seen all the television shows. Hercules is my favorite actor—after you, of course."

"I'm sure Hercules is a little tired of traveling in the truck," Pierre Beeswax, also known as Sergeant Schwartz of the Yukon, said. "I'll go and get him."

"Norman! Bruce! He's going to get the great dog Hercules!" Steve was really excited. "Norman, put down a bowl of fresh water! Hercules might be thirsty. Maybe we should go and get Edward—he wouldn't want to miss this . . . . . . Ooooooh! Look! Isn't he beautiful!"

Pierre Beeswax/Sergeant Schwartz had opened the back door of the truck and lifted out a big Malamute. He was about fifty pounds overweight. He was smiling, and his tongue was hanging out. It looked as though he didn't have many teeth.

Hercules stumbled around the restaurant, dabbed each of our hands with his tongue, took a drink of water, and thumped to the floor. In a minute he was sleeping.

"Old Hercules is a little bit out of condition," Sergeant Schwartz/Pierre Beeswax said.

"Oh, no! He's beautiful," Steve said. "This is the proudest day of my life. But I'm being rude. These are my friends, Norman Bleistift and Bruce the milkman."

We shook hands with the actor.

"And I'm Steve Nickelson. Now may I offer you some refreshment—my treat, of course."

"I'd be delighted," Schwartz/Beeswax said. "I was just looking at all these handsome signs. What, for example, is a Moron's Delight?"

"My masterpiece!" Steve said. "It's a meal, a snack, and a course in practical nutrition all in one. It would be a supreme honor to make one for you—and one for Hercules, in case he wakes up."

Steve whipped together two Moron's Delights, three times normal size. Beeswax/ Schwartz went right to work on his. The great dog Hercules accepted the treat and lapped at it without getting off the floor.

"Mr. Beeswax," I asked, "were you ever a real mountie?"

"An interesting question, young Norman Bleistift," he said. "I *could* have been a real mountie. You see, when the

producers of Sergeant Schwartz of the Yukon were looking for an actor to play the role, they wanted someone
who met all the physical, mental, and moral requirements
of the Northwest Constabulary. In fact, since he was going
to portray a Mountie, the actor had to be more like all the
mounties than any one mountie could be in real life. He
had to embody all that was good, brave, and true about
those good, brave, and true men of the north. And they
picked me—a good choice, don't you think?"

"The best choice," Steve said. "And the best choice of
dog to play Hercules, too."

"In fact, I *am* an honorary mountie," Pierre Beeswax
continued, "and I am a natural detective. If my gifts as an
actor had not been so great, I might have been a mountie,
and I'm sure I would have done at least as well as the
character I portrayed."

"Sergeant Schwartz, I have a surprise for you," Steve
said. "My dog, who took all the prizes at the dog show, is
a grandson of Hercules."

"No fooling?" Beeswax said. "I'd be pleased to meet
him."

"He's just out back," Steve said. "I'll go and get him." He
started for the back door and paused. "I'm sure if Hercules
had been there on time, *he* would have won."

"Naturally," said Pierre Beeswax/Sergeant Schwartz.

We heard Steve whistling and calling in the alley. Then
he came back into the Magic Moscow. He was very pale.
"Edward is gone!" he said.

6

Sergeant Beeswax jumped to his feet and rushed out the back door. We all crowded after him. In the alley, he got down on all fours and pulled a magnifying glass out of his back pocket. He examined various scraps of dirt and garbage. Then he jumped to his feet and sniffed the air, licked one finger and held it up to test the wind, and turned to Steve. "Dog rustlers!" he said.

"Dog rustlers?"

"Yes," Pierre Schwartz answered. "My contacts in the police tell me that a band of desperadoes, named Slade, Blackie, and Nick, are operating in this area. I have no doubt that they are the ones who have purloined your prize sled dog. He's worth his weight in gold, you know."

"He is?" Steve asked.

"Certainly," Sergeant Pierre said. "Everybody knows that a dog is man's best friend—well, a good sled dog can mean the difference between life and death on the trail. It is my conviction that these three scoundrels, Nick, Blackie, and Slade, will take your dog to the north country and sell him for a king's ransom."

"Oh, no!" Steve said, "we've got to stop them! Let's call the police!"

"That won't be necessary," Sergeant Schwartz said. "Don't forget, *I* am here. We will pursue them at once."

We hurried through the Magic Moscow. Sergeant Schwartz called to his sleeping dog, "Up, Hercules. Up, you Malamute!" The dog snored. "Oh, drat!" Sergeant Schwartz said, and gathered the huge dog up in his arms and carried him out to the truck, still sleeping. "He's the very devil in a fight," the sergeant said. "If the rascals try to resist, Hercules will be all over them."

Sergeant Schwartz's truck refused to start.

"I'll get my horse!" Bruce the milkman said.

"Good!" Sergeant Schwartz said. "They won't be expecting a horse."

In a few minutes, Bruce the milkman galloped up in the milk wagon. I was impressed. I had never seen Cheryl gallop. In fact, I would never have dreamed that she could gallop.

Hercules was still sleeping off his Moron's Delight. He burped as we transferred him from the back of Sergeant Schwartz's stalled truck to the milk wagon.

"That way! There's no time to lose!" Sergeant Schwartz shouted.

Bruce the milkman clucked his tongue and Cheryl started off at a fast trot. She wasn't about to gallop with three men, a kid, and a fat dog on board.

"How do you know which way they went?" Steve asked.

"Mountie intuition," the sergeant said. "Now keep a sharp lookout. They could be anywhere."

We trotted through the streets of Hoboken. Every now and then, Sergeant Schwartz would say, "Sharp left here!" or, "Turn right, Constable Bruce!" In his excitement, he seemed to think we were all mounties. Sometimes he'd shout, "On! On, you Malamutes!" In between he'd hum the theme music from the "Sergeant Schwartz of the Yukon" televison show.

"Slade, Nick, and Blackie are masters of disguise," the sergeant said, "and it's possible that they've disguised your dog, too. Don't let anything suspicious escape your notice. It's too bad I don't have my revolver. But we've got

Hercules in the back. If they put up a fight, he'll surprise them." Sergeant Schwartz chuckled. Hercules burped.

We only had one false alarm. Sergeant Schwartz stopped a car with four fat ladies in it and accused them of being Slade, Nick, and Blackie with Edward dressed up as a fat lady. Steve managed to calm them down by promising them free Moron's Delights at the Magic Moscow.

Then we sighted Edward! He was trotting down the street, following a little girl who was eating a tuna-fish sandwich as she walked.

Bruce the milkman reined Cheryl to a stop, and Sergeant Schwartz leaped out of the wagon.

"So Blackie, Slade, and Nick are working with an accomplice!" the sergeant said. "Clever of them to use a little girl. Stand still, little girl," he bellowed. "Don't go for your gun, I warn you."

Steve grabbed Edward and put him in the milk wagon. Hercules opened one eye, looked at his grandson, and went back to sleep.

Edward hopped into his customary seat and barked hello to his friend, Cheryl.

Sergeant Schwartz warned the little girl to give up her life of crime. He tried to get her to tell him where Nick, Slade, and Blackie were hiding, but she wouldn't talk. She just chewed on her tuna-fish sandwich and looked at the sergeant as if he were crazy.

Finally we went back to the Magic Moscow.

The four fat ladies Sergeant Schwartz had tried to arrest were there waiting for their free Moron's Delights.

The sergeant, Hercules, and Edward all had Moron's Delights, too, while Bruce the milkman found the loose wire in Sergeant Schwartz's truck and got it started.

Finally, everybody shook hands: Steve, Bruce the milkman, me, Sergeant Schwartz, the four fat ladies, and Edward. Hercules had dozed off the middle of his second Moron's Delight and had to be carried to the truck.

Sergeant Schwartz loaded Hercules into the front seat and climbed in beside him. "Hercules," he said to the half-asleep dog, "this case is closed."

Then Sergeant Schwartz switched on a tape deck, which played the theme music from the "Sergeant Schwartz of the Yukon" television show, put the truck into gear, and drove off into the sunset over Jersey City.

ATTILA THE PUN

A MAGIC MOSCOW STORY

This is a sequel to The Magic Moscow. *It is a silly—I should say sillier-than-usual—story, so much so that I can think of very little to say about it. Except this: If there were ever a place where you'd be likely to meet an ancient Hun ghost, it is Hoboken. Hoboken is a port. Ships come in from everywhere. In the streets of Hoboken you might hear 50 languages spoken, and see people from every country you've ever heard of. You would also see people from places you've never heard of.*

I'm talking about Lascars, Dyaks, Copper Eskimos—ever heard of them? Also, in addition to every race, nationality, and ethnic group, Hoboken had more than its share of weird and strange people. I haven't been back lately, but I'll bet you can still find them there.

1

Nobody has a room like mine. It's the whole basement of our house on River Street. A long time ago, before we lived in the house, somebody made the basement into a sort of indoor beer garden, with paintings on all the walls. Actually, it's just one painting that goes all around the walls—a mural. It shows green hills, lakes with sail-boats, trees and flowers, and lots of grapevines.

There are little light fixtures in the ceiling, covered with pieces of colored glass. There is a panel with ten switches to control the lights. You can get all red lights, or red and blue, or blue and green. The mural looks really good with the blue-and-green-colored lights on.

At one end of my basement, there's a bar. I made that into my desk. I just pulled one of the tall stools behind the bar and put my lamp on it—and there was my desk. There are plenty of shelves behind the bar and under it. It makes a great place to write and do homework. And, get this, there's a little tiny refrigerator under the bar, where I can keep cold orange juice and stuff.

Of course, there isn't a whole lot of daylight in my room. All that gets through the four little windows up near the ceiling is enough to make the mural look like twilight in the forest. That doesn't bother me; if I want sunshine, I can go outside. If I drag one of the barstools up to one of the little windows, I can crawl out. Of course, I can just go up the stairs and out the front door too—but I can sneak out the window without anybody knowing it.

The best thing about my room is its size. I have room for just about anything. If I find something, no matter how big it is, I can take it back to my room. For example, I have an actual stuffed moose head. That's something I found. It had one antler broken off. I dragged it home and wrapped the broken antler with friction tape. It sags a little, but the moose head still looks great.

Another thing I found was an old-time record player. It's the kind you wind with a crank. It's on wheels, so I rolled it home. The whole thing is about as tall as me, and there's a sort of cabinet in front. I found a bunch of really old records in it. The record player didn't work at first, but I squirted some oil here and there, and now it works fine.

It's amazing what you can find on the street in Hoboken. You just have to keep a sharp lookout—and have some-place to take what you find.

I have a family, of course, but they don't come down to my room much. My mother says it's disgusting. She doesn't like the moose head: She says it must have fleas. I am responsible for my own cleaning and I keep the room nice. I don't care what my mother says.

It's just my mother and father and me at home. I have a married sister. She lives in Idaho, on a farm with a lot of other people. It's a communal farm, which means they all work together and share everything. She calls home once in a while to ask for money. Her husband is sort of a neat guy. His name is Ron. They have three kids named Sun, Moon, and Beancurd. Once a year they all visit us. They're relaxing people to have around. They meditate. My father says they're harmless.

My sister's name is Louise. She's okay. I also have an older brother. His name is Neil. I'm sorry to say, Neil is a jerk. He thinks he's wonderful. I don't know why. When Neil comes home, he always wants to go out in the street and throw a ball back and forth with me. This goes on for about fifteen minutes. The rest of the time he ignores me. Neil and Louise are both a good deal older than me; we haven't got much in common.

I have a cat named Arthur. Arthur is strictly *my* cat. There's nobody else he likes. Arthur happens to be one of the smartest cats in history. He comes and goes through one of the windows. He's orange, and he has bad breath. He's an outstanding cat. He really likes me. He also likes the old jazz records I found with the windup record player. When I play them, Arthur rubs against the legs of the machine. Arthur's favorite record—and mine—is called "West End Blues" by Louis Armstrong.

2

Someone else who likes old records is Steve Nickelson. Steve is my friend. He is also my boss. He runs the Magic Moscow.

The Magic Moscow is mainly an ice-cream stand—but Steve also sells hamburgers, carrot juice, and bean-sprout salad. Steve is divided in his love for health food and fattening junk.

Steve collects comic books, old records, pennies, bottle caps, antique sneakers, and all sorts of things. He also has a dog named Edward who lives in the Magic Moscow, since Steve's parents won't let him in their house.

My part-time job is helping Steve in the Magic Moscow, but sometimes I get to help him with his collections. We both take care of Edward.

In the summer, I work full time for Steve. My parents say I don't have to do that. They say I could go to camp or just hang out with the other kids, but I'd rather work. During the school term, when I'm only working part time, I'm always afraid I'll miss something at the Magic Moscow. All sorts of interesting things happen and all sorts of interesting people come in while I'm in school.

In the summer, I'm at the Magic Moscow from the time it opens until the time it closes—that's thirteen hours a day—so I don't miss a thing.

I also make huge sums of money working all those hours. I think there's a law that says a kid can't work more than eight hours, but I do anyway. Of course, Steve lets me goof off any time I want to. I can go into the restaurant part of the Magic Moscow and sit around and read, or talk to my friends. The restaurant part of the Magic Moscow used to be a parking lot. Then he put a roof over it and set up picnic tables; next he put walls around it—and it became a restaurant. I helped Steve put posters and comic book covers up all around the walls. After my room, it's the neatest place in town.

3

O ne time, Steve left me in charge of the Magic Moscow, while he went to see about buying some telephones. He had taken to buying up all sorts of telephones, old and new. Another collection.

I had run the Magic Moscow all by myself lots of times. In the evening, Steve would close up the restaurant and turn off the grill. Then we'd just sell ice cream through the little window to people in the street.

It was a cool evening. There wouldn't be a lot of business. I could handle it. Steve had left a stack of Django Reinhardt records behind the counter, and I was playing them on the old phonograph he keeps in the store.

A couple of kids came by for one-scoop cones with sprinkles, and a family pulled up in a car, all wanting strawberry milkshakes. Easy.

For a long time, nobody came. Nobody even passed by. I sat on a stool near the little window, listening to Django and leafing through an old copy of *Stupefying Science Fiction*. The Magic Moscow has these yellow fluorescent lights. They're supposed to repel bugs, but what they really do is make it impossible to enjoy comic books. They kill the color.

Then, the scariest guy I'd ever seen appeared at the little window.

He was about seven feet tall. He had a big black slouch hat and a loose black coat that reached all the way to the ground. He had a long, really incredibly long, nose. And he had strange eyes. In the shadow of the hat, about all I could see of him was his nose and those eyes! They seemed to be glowing, like a gas flame.

For a long time, the tall scary guy just stood there, not saying a word. I couldn't look away from those eyes. I couldn't feel the floor under my feet. It was hard to breathe.

Finally, he spoke. I could breathe. I felt the floor under my sneakers. The spell was broken.

"Can you fix me a Nuclear Meltdown to go?" the tall scary guy asked.

A Nuclear Meltdown is one of Steve's specialties. It has nine flavors of ice cream, a sliced radish, a peach, four kinds of syrup, sunflower seeds, bran flakes, a slice of baked ham, and a pickled tomato. The whole thing is served on top of three whole-wheat English muffins and covered with swiss cheese. Just before serving it, you put it under the broiler for a couple of minutes to get the cheese melting. It comes in a big cardboard bucket.

I didn't say a word. I made the Nuclear Meltdown and slid it across the counter, through the little window, to the tall scary guy. He slid a five-dollar bill toward me. I rang up the Nuclear Meltdown and slid his change—five cents—back through the little window. Then he was gone. I felt cold sweat trickle down my back.

Who was that guy?

4

C alm down, Norman," Steve said. "You're so excited, I can't understand what you're trying to tell me."

I guess I was excited. The weird guy with the glowing eyes had upset me more than I thought. When Steve walked in with a carton full of dusty princess phones, I started bombarding him with questions about the scary stranger.

Steve fixed me a carrot fizz—that's carrot juice, raspberry syrup, and soda water. As I drank it, I slowed down a bit and asked my questions one at a time.

"You must have seen Lamont Penumbra," Steve said. "He's a regular customer. I'm surprised you never saw him before. He's really a nice fellow. He gives lessons of some sort in a loft over the Puerto Rican restaurant on Washington Street."

"He scared me," I said. "He looked so evil! Did you know that his eyes glow in the dark?"

"Look," Steve said, "it's wrong to judge people by the way they look. Lamont Penumbra is a nice guy, I promise you. In fact, I think we ought to go up to his loft, and I'll introduce you to him. Then you'll see that he's no one to be afraid of."

"Go to his loft? Go where he lives?"

"Sure," Steve said. "I've been up there any number of times. Very often, when he's too busy to come down here, he telephones me, and I deliver a Nuclear Meltdown on my way home after closing time. He has at least one a day. He's a person of taste and culture."

I wasn't at all sure I wanted to go with Steve to visit Lamont Penumbra's loft.

"Let's close up early," Steve said. "I don't think we'll get any more customers tonight. We'll clean up fast and then go over to Lamont Penumbra's."

"Uh . . . I don't think we should just barge in on him," I said. I really didn't want to go and visit that scary guy. I was still feeling a tingling in the soles of my feet, left over from his visit to the Magic Moscow.

"It will be all right," Steve said. "I tell you, he's a very friendly guy."

5

There were lots of people in the Parthenon Puerto Rican Restaurant. They were talking and laughing and drinking cups of coffee and listening to the juke box and eating sandwiches and plates of roast meat, rice, and inky black beans. Good smells drifted out into the street. It was bright and friendly looking inside the restaurant.

Next to the Parthenon Puerto Rican Restaurant was a doorway. We went in. There was a long flight of dimly lit stairs. It looked as though it went up forever. Everything was greenish and had an underwater look. There were little, dim light bulbs, placed at long intervals along the stairs. They barely gave any light.

We started to climb.

"Are you sure we aren't being rude, coming here without any warning?" I asked.

"It will be all right," Steve said. "You'll see."

We climbed a long way. We passed a few tiny landings with black doors, opening onto apartments or lofts, I supposed. I didn't have the feeling that anybody lived behind those doors. If one had opened suddenly, I would have screamed.

Lamont Penumbra's door was all the way at the top of the stairs. It was a big black-painted door, like the others, but it had neat white-stenciled letters on it: L. PENUMBRA, MYSTIC SEER.

"Mystic seer?" I asked.

"Mystic seer," Steve answered.

He knocked.

"Yes?" I recognized the voice of the guy with the glowing eyes.

"It's Steve Nickelson, from the Magic Moscow—and my helper, Norman Bleistift. We thought we'd drop by to say hello."

"Hello?" said the voice from behind the door.

"Yes—we thought we'd visit you, if that's all right."

"All right," said the voice.

"Uh . . . may we come in?" Steve asked.

"Come in!" the voice said.

Steve pushed the door. It opened into a huge room. It was much, much bigger than my room. It was as big as a basketball court. The room appeared to be mostly empty. It was also mostly dark. At the far end of the room was Lamont Penumbra, sitting under a blue light.

"Kindly approach," he said. "It was nice of you to think of visiting me."

We made our way down the length of the dark room, heading for the blue light and Lamont Penumbra.

When we had arrived at the little table, Lamont Penumbra indicated a couple of chairs, half-visible in the gloom outside the circle of light from his blue lamp. We dragged the chairs closer to the little table and sat down.

Lamont Penumbra was wearing the long black coat and the black broad-brimmed slouch hat he'd been wearing in the street. His face was in shadow, and all we could see was the tip of his enormous nose and the dim blue glow of his eyes.

"You are visitors, is that right?" he asked.

"Yes," Steve said, "visitors."

"You are not seekers?"

"Seekers?" Steve asked. "What's that?"

I was impressed by the way that Steve didn't seem nervous at all. I, myself, was plenty scared of Lamont

Penumbra. Steve's idea that visiting him would help me get over being scared was not working out.

"Seekers," Lamont Penumbra said. "Seekers after mystical truths, students of the occult, persons desiring to learn the ancient wisdom—you're none of those?"

"No," Steve said. "We just wanted to visit."

"In that case," said Lamont Penumbra, "let's get some light on the subject."

He flipped a switch, and ceiling lights came on—regular ones. The blue gloom was gone. Lamont Penumbra also took off his hat and long black coat, revealing himself as bald and very tall and skinny. He was wearing a yellow T-shirt with a picture of a wave on it and the slogan *I'd Rather Be Surfing.*

"You guys want a cup of tea?" Lamont Penumbra asked.

6

M r. Penumbra," Steve began.
"Call me Lamont."

"Lamont," Steve continued, "Norman and I were talking about you a while ago, and I was telling him that I never did know just what it is you do."

"Do?"

"Yes. I mean, what's a mystic seer?"

"Oh, you mean my profession," Lamont Penumbra said. "Well, as a mystic seer I do a number of things. I cast horoscopes, read palms, read tarot cards, give mystical advice, and answer questions. I can also chase ghosts, if you have them, and tell things about what will happen to you by feeling the bumps on your head."

"So you're a fortune-teller," Steve said.

"That's it," Lamont Penumbra said.

"I never believed in any of that stuff, myself," Steve said.

"Neither do I," Lamont Penumbra said.

"You don't believe in it?" Steve asked. "You mean you're a fake?"

"Well—sort of," Lamont Penumbra said.

"Isn't that dishonest?" Steve asked.

"Not really," Lamont Penumbra said. "I honestly tell my customers what they want to hear. I try not to tell any big lies. The only thing that's a tiny bit dishonest is that I don't tell them that the horoscopes and so forth are nonsense. Of course, if they were to ask me, I'd tell them—but they never ask."

"Mr. Penumbra," I said.

"Call me Lamont."

"Lamont." I went on, "If you are a fake fortune-teller, how are you able to make your eyes glow like they did when you came to the Magic Moscow earlier? I was really scared."

"There are tricks to every trade," Lamont Penumbra said. "The idea isn't so much to scare you as to impress people. I wouldn't be very good as a mystic seer if I couldn't impress people."

By this time, I wasn't feeling very afraid of Lamont Penumbra at all. He was just a nice middle-aged hippie. The teakettle began to whistle, and he busied himself making a pot of tea for us. It smelled of mint.

"This is very interesting," Steve said. "I've never met a mystic seer before. Is it the same as a wizard?"

"I only wish it was," Lamont Penumbra said. "A wizard! That's what I started out to be. Somehow everything I studied in the wizard line turned out to be either a fraud or something which did not work at all. I always wanted to be a real magician, but I was never able to learn any real magic. I'm not even sure if there is such a thing anymore. So I make my living by telling people that they are going to be rich and happy by feeling the bumps on their heads. On Saturday nights, I put on a gypsy suit and tell fortunes in the restaurant downstairs in exchange for a free meal. It's really very depressing when I think about it."

Lamont Penumbra looked very depressed as he sipped his mint-flavored tea.

"I didn't mean to bring up any sensitive subjects," Steve said. "I hope you aren't mad at us."

"No, no! Not at all," Lamont Penumbra said. "It's really very nice to have visitors who aren't interested in having their fortunes told. Everybody who comes up here wants me to do their horoscope and tell them they're going to be rich and happy. It's nice to have regular visitors for a change."

"You know," Steve said, "I purchased a large private library recently that had a lot of magical books in it. I, myself, am only interested in comic books and science fiction. The magical books look very old. Maybe you'd like to have them."

"That's very kind of you," Lamont Penumbra said.

"I'll have Norman bring them up tomorrow," Steve said.

7

The next day, Steve gave me a carton of old books to take to Lamont Penumbra's loft.

I climbed the stairs. They were just as dark by day as they had been the night before. When I came to Lamont Penumbra's door, with the stenciled white letters, L. PENUMBRA, MYSTIC SEER, I knocked.

"Yes?"

"It's me," I said. "Norman Bleistift. I was here last night with Steve Nickelson."

"Here?" asked the voice from behind the door.

"Yes," I said, "we were here. I've got the books Steve told you about."

"Books?"

"Yes. May I come in?"

"Come in."

I pushed the door open with the carton of books. I wasn't surprised to see that Lamont Penumbra's loft was just as dark as it had been the previous night. There he was, wearing his black hat and coat, sitting by the blue light.

"Approach," he said.

I approached, "Look, Mr. Penumbra. . . ."

"Call me Lamont."

"Look, Lamont, it's just me, Norman. I've got the magical books Steve promised you. You don't have to go through this whole routine with the blue light and all."

"You are all alone?" Lamont Penumbra asked. "This crummy blue light is ruining my eyesight. I wouldn't want a potential customer to come in here and catch me out of character. Now, let's have a look at the books."

The books in the carton were all pretty old. The oldest-looking ones were stubby and fat, printed on thick yellow paper that was wavy like potato chips and bound in smooth white leather that was all smudged and black at the corners and on the spine. There were other old books, bound in red and black leather and stamped in gold. There were quite a few books in the carton.

"Look at this," Lamont Penumbra said. "This is some pretty good stuff!" He pulled out one of the volumes. "*Malleus Malificarum!* An oldie but a goodie! Here's another classic, *Die Magie als Naturwissenschaft.* And what have we here?" Lamont Penumbra was obviously having a good time. "Here's one I never heard of, *Natura Magicum Phantomium*, and another, *The Experiments of Istvan of Budapest.* These are all good books! And here's the good old *Sorcerer's Guide!*

"Norman, please tell Steve that I am very grateful for this box of books. They're really wonderful! I'll come down and thank him in person later—but now, if you'll excuse me, I want to start reading some of these right away."

With that, Lamont Penumbra began diving into first one book and then another, mumbling and licking his fingers as he leafed through pages. He'd read a little of one book and then grab another, riffling through it until he found something interesting, and then grab another, and so on. He took no notice of me. After a while, I tiptoed out and quietly closed the door. He was still flipping through one book after another and mumbling to himself.

I went back to the Magic Moscow and told Steve that Lamont Penumbra was having a good time with the books he had sent. Then I went in the back and put a few pounds of carrots through the juicer for the noon rush.

8

Steve was running a special on The Hungarian Boy Scout Lunch. It cost a dollar seventy-five. It consisted of two cold, cooked hot dogs, two slices of rye bread, a chocolate bar, and a pack of cigarettes. The idea was that you took it with you to the park and had a picnic. "This is what Hungarian Boy Scouts always take with them on hikes," Steve said.

It didn't seem likely that all Hungarian Boy Scouts smoked cigarettes. Also, it didn't seem like much of a lunch to me. Apparently, nobody thought so either, because Steve hardly sold any all day.

Steve couldn't understand it. He had about three dozen Hungarian Boy Scout Lunches all made up and standing on the counter in brown paper bags. In the end, Steve made me eat Hungarian Boy Scout Lunches all that week. Edward refused to even sniff them. Steve smoked the cigarettes.

The weather got warmer, and the ice-cream business picked up. There were lots of people out strolling at night, and there were long lines under the yellow fluorescent lights.

It was a normal week.

We hadn't seen Lamont Penumbra for quite a few days after I had taken him the box of magical books.

He turned up on a warm afternoon. He was wearing his black coat and hat as usual. There was sweat dripping from the end of his nose.

Lamont Penumbra pushed five fat candles through the little window. "Take these," he said, "and put them in a circle on the floor; light them at midnight. I've got a great surprise for you." Then he hurried off, his black coat flapping behind him.

Steve put the candles on the shelf where he keeps the paper napkins and straws. That night, at five minutes to midnight, after closing time, he put each candle on a paper plate, stuck to it with a little drip of wax, and lighted them in a circle on the floor.

The phone rang. It was Lamont Penumbra. "Did you light the candles?" he asked.

"We just lighted them," I said.

"Okay. Good. Now, just sit down and watch the middle of the circle," Lamont Penumbra said over the phone. "You're going to see something really fantastic in a few minutes."

I told Steve what Lamont Penumbra had said. We pulled up chairs and sat down, watching the flickering candles.

Nothing happened.

About fifteen minutes went by. The candles flickered. The refrigerators hummed. Edward snored. Steve smoked cigarettes left over from the Hungarian Boy Scout Lunches.

The candles were about a quarter burned. They were smoking a lot.

"Maybe we ought to turn out the lights," I said.

"Okay," Steve said, and he did it.

Neither of us said anything. We sat in chairs and waited for Lamont Penumbra's fantastic trick to come off.

It never did.

After about a half-hour, when the candles were burned halfway down, the phone rang. It was Lamont again.

This time Steve answered. "Did you see anything?" Lamont Penumbra asked.

"Like what?" Steve wanted to know.

"Anything unusual," Lamont Penumbra said.

"No," Steve said, "we just watched the candles. It was very restful."

"Oh, rats!" Lamont Penumbra said. "You mean you didn't see anything amazing? Anything magical?"

"No," Steve said. "But I did have an amazing thought."

"Like a vision? What was it?" Lamont Penumbra asked.

"Well, I'm going to get those red glass things with candles in them and put them on all the tables," Steve said. "Then, at night we'll light them. You can get them with insect-repellent candles, so they'll keep the mosquitoes away, besides making the place look very nice."

There was a long silence on the phone. Finally, Lamont Penumbra said, "Look, I'm very depressed. Do you think you might come up here and maybe bring me a Nuclear Meltdown? I need cheering up."

"Will do," Steve said and hung up.

9

I had never actually watched anyone eat a Nuclear Meltdown. It was a spectacular sight. Lamont Penumbra dug into the gigantic, gloppy, gooey mess with enthusiasm.

Steve and I munched on the last two Hungarian Boy Scout Lunches, which we had brought along. I was glad they were the last. The cold hot dogs were all shriveled up and nasty looking after a whole week in the back of the refrigerator.

As he mopped up the last of the Nuclear Meltdown, Lamont Penumbra said, "Well, it happened again—rather, it didn't happen again. It's the story of my life."

"I don't quite follow," Steve said. "What are you talking about?"

"The experiment," Lamont Penumbra said, "with the five candles. I was sure it would work. I was supposed to appear in the middle of the circle—at least my image was supposed to appear. You're sure you didn't see anything?"

"Nothing," Steve said.

"And you were watching?"

"Intently."

"I don't know why I don't just give up," Lamont Penumbra said. "I really thought I had it this time. Some of those old magic books you gave me really looked like the genuine article. I wanted you to see the first real magic I'd ever done, because you gave me the books."

"Did you read all the books?" I asked.

"Not all of them," Lamont Penumbra said, "but the ones I read had some fantastic spells in them. I can't understand why it didn't work."

"Don't get discouraged," Steve said. "Magic must be very hard to do; otherwise, everybody would do it. Maybe you picked a spell that was too difficult, or maybe you made a little mistake."

"Or maybe I just don't have any real talent," Lamont Penumbra said.

"I'm sure you have talent," Steve said, "but you picked a very difficult trick. I mean, appearing in the middle of a circle of candles three blocks away—that has to be something very advanced."

"Well, I followed the instructions exactly as they were written in the book," Lamont Penumbra said. "The only thing I didn't have was powdered unicorn horn to make the candles with, so I used moth flakes. Do you suppose a little thing like that could make the spell go wrong?"

"Of course!" Steve said. "That has to be it. You can't work with inferior materials. That's why the olive milk shake I invented last month was a failure—I used canned olives. You have to get good stuff, if you want good results."

"Maybe you're right," Lamont Penumbra said, "but then things are just as hopeless. You have no idea how many ingredients are simply impossible to get. Unicorn horn is just one of them. The witchcraft supply house in New York City doesn't have half the things I need."

"Aren't there any easy spells in any of the books?" I asked. "I mean, aren't there any tricks that don't require hard-to-get stuff?" I had always thought that magicians, if they really existed, could make things happen just by saying magic words or maybe waving a magic wand. I never knew they needed unicorn horn or anything like that."

"There are some easy spells," Lamont Penumbra said, "but they aren't very interesting. For example, there's a spell for making a razor blade last twice as long as normal. And there's a spell for ensuring that no one will steal your shoes while you're asleep, and one against people putting poison in your well, and one against having a horseshoe fall on your head from a great height. You see? Spells like that may have been useful at one time, but they aren't much fun."

"Isn't there something sort of in-between?" Steve asked.

"Well, I found one spell that was kind of cute," Lamont Penumbra said, "and it doesn't require any special equipment or ingredients. It's one that makes a person able to summon the ghost of a famous person from history."

"Which famous person?" Steve asked.

"The spell doesn't say," Lamont Penumbra said, "and . . . I just remembered, there's a catch to that one. It only works on people less than sixty inches in height. I'm six foot six—that's seventy-eight inches."

"I'm six feet tall myself," Steve said, "but Norman might be less than sixty inches. Can the spell work for someone else?"

"I suppose so," Lamont Penumbra said. "How tall are you, Norman?"

"I don't know exactly," I said. "I've been doing a lot of growing lately."

"Stand up straight against this wall," Lamont Penumbra said. He made a mark on the wall with a pencil. Then he rummaged around and found a ruler. "Rats!" he said. "I make this fifty-nine and seven-eights inches. I don't think it will work—that's pretty close to sixty."

"But you measured him with his shoes on," Steve said. "Does the book say whether the spell will work on someone less than sixty inches tall with his shoes on or less than sixty inches tall with his shoes off? Besides, Norman is an eighth of an inch under the mark, even with his shoes on. Let's give the spell a try."

"All right," Lamont Penumbra said, "but I don't expect it to work."

Lamont Penumbra had me take my shoes off, just to be on the safe side, and stand in the middle of the room.

"Now this won't hurt a bit," Lamont Penumbra said. "You don't have to do anything. Just stand there with your eyes closed and think pleasant thoughts. While you do that, I am going to go into a mystic trance, and then I'll throw a sort of fit. Don't be alarmed, or take any notice of what I do. Just stand there, thinking pleasant thoughts. After a while, you will feel the irresistible urge to bark like a dog, mew like a cat, neigh like a horse, honk like a goose, hiss like a snake, and so forth. Just go ahead and do those things—don't be afraid that you'll appear foolish. You won't appear any more foolish than I will. When I say 'stop' you will stop barking, mewing, neighing, honking, hissing, and so on. Then the ghost of a famous person from history will appear and talk to us. Is that okay with you?"

I said it was.

"You're doing this very well, Lamont," Steve said.

"Thank you," Lamont Penumbra said. "Now, let's get started."

I stood in the middle of the room with my shoes off. I tried to think pleasant thoughts. The best one I could come up with was being in a rented rowboat in the little lake in North Hudson Park. That's something I often think about just as I fall asleep.

Meanwhile, Lamont Penumbra went into a mystic trance. At least, I suppose he did—my eyes were closed.

Then he had his fit, just as he said he would. It was hard to keep my eyes closed. I really wanted to peek and see what he was doing. I could hear him thumping around the room and muttering strange things. Later, Steve told me that he had been hopping around the room on one foot—backward.

He was mumbling something like, "Waka hakakabakka kawakaka baka waka waka hakakawaka."

Everything went according to plan—except that I did not bark, nor mew, nor neigh. Neither did I honk or hiss like a snake. Mostly I just stood there feet bare and eyes closed. It must have gone on for half an hour.

"Did you feel anything?" Lamont Penumbra asked me.

"No." I was embarrassed. I felt sorry for Lamont Penumbra. I wished that I had felt an irresistible urge to bark at least once. But, I hadn't felt a thing, except bored and foolish.

"Oh, rats! Double rats!" Lamont Penumbra said. "I'm so depressed! I don't want to live anymore!"

I felt terrible. I felt as though I had let Lamont Penumbra down. "I really tried," I said.

"We know you did," Steve said, "but it's getting late. Maybe you should go home before your parents get worried. I'll stay with Lamont and make sure he doesn't hurt himself. Maybe we'll go out for a pizza."

As I left the loft, I could hear Lamont Penumbra saying, "Rats! Rats! Double rats!" and Steve saying, "You like anchovies?"

10

My parents are late-movie freaks. They're always up until at least two in the morning, so it's no big deal when I come home from the Magic Moscow after midnight—in the summer, that is.

They were watching the movie where Anthony Quinn plays an Eskimo when I got home. I said hello to them and went downstairs to my room.

Arthur was sleeping in the middle of my bed. I picked him up and put him on a chair. He half woke up and gave me one raspy lick. Then he started snoring again. He's the only cat I know of who snores.

I kicked my shoes off.

In the middle of unbuttoning my shirt, I stood in the middle of my room and closed my eyes.

Without meaning to, or wanting to, I barked once—then a lot of times. Then I miaowed, whinnied, honked like a goose, and hissed like a snake.

"Stop all that noise and go to bed!" my father shouted from upstairs.

"That was the silliest performance I've ever seen," someone else said. There was someone in my room!

Arthur was wide awake and staring at a point behind me as though he were looking at a ghost.

I felt a tingling all over my body. Lamont Penumbra's spell had worked after all! It had worked! Somehow the working of the spell had been delayed for a while—and now, there was a ghost in my room! Behind me was the ghost of some famous person from history. I was scared. Arthur was making a low moaning noise, and all his fur was standing straight up.

"Are you a ghost?" I asked unsteadily.

"I am a ghost," the voice behind me said, "a spirit summoned here by your incantation."

"Are you the ghost of a famous person from history?" I asked.

"Yes," said the voice. "I am the ghost of Alexander Hamilton, first secretary of the treasury of the United States. I was killed in a duel in 1804, just across the town line in Weehawken."

I pulled myself together. Alexander Hamilton wasn't scary. I'd read about him in school. I turned slowly and faced the ghost.

Never having seen a ghost before, I didn't know quite what to expect. What I saw was quite a surprise. For one thing, it wasn't someone wrapped in a white sheet or glowing like a neon light. What I saw was a short guy, with a snub nose and tangled gray hair. He was wearing some kind of fur thing over his shoulders, and his arms were bare. He was sort of dark in coloring and had big muscles. On his head, the ghost had a leather helmet with a point on top, and he was wearing a sort of short skirt made of plates of iron. On his feet he had rags wrapped with rope, and he was holding a big sword.

"You're not Alexander Hamilton!" I said, before I knew what I was doing. I had seen a picture of Alexander Hamilton in my history book, and he didn't look anything like this.

"No," the ghost said. "In fact, I am not Alexander Hamilton. I just said that for a joke. The truth is, I am really the ghost of Frank Sinatra."

"I've seen Frank Sinatra on television," I said, "and you're not him. Besides, I don't think he's even dead."

"Look," the ghost said, "why did you summon me if you just want to argue?"

"I don't want to argue," I said, "and it wasn't really me that summoned you. It was this guy, Lamont Penumbra . . . who are you really?"

"Look at me!" the ghost said. "Do you really mean to say that you don't know who I am?"

I looked at the ghost. He looked pretty scruffy. Also, he smelled of horses. I never knew that you could smell a ghost. "I give up," I said. "Who are you?"

"I am Attila!" the ghost said.

I knew who that was! "No kidding?" I said. "Are you really Attila, the Hun, the Scourge of God? The guy who subjugated Europe in the fifth century? Who engaged in all kinds of battles, raised huge armies, and rode all over the place, putting cities and people to the torch?" This had been one of my favorite parts of the history book.

"Well, to be absolutely truthful," the ghost said, "no, I'm not. If you want to know, I'm Attila's brother, Bleda. Someone accidentally chopped my head off with a sword in the year 445. It still comes off—want to see?" The ghost made a gesture, offering to remove his head for me.

"No thanks," I said, "please keep your head on." I was surprised to find that I wasn't too terribly scared of this ghost, but I really didn't want to see him take his head off.

"You can call me Attila," he said. "People used to call me Attila—but they didn't call me Attila the Hun."

"What did they call you?" I asked.

"They called me . . . Attila the Pun!" the ghost said. "When is a door not a door? When it's ajar! When is a door ready to eat? When it's jammed! Why did the toast rise to the ceiling? Because butter flies! What do jokers eat for breakfast? Puns and coffee!" Then he started laughing and staggered around the room, howling and slapping his legs with his hands. He really thought he was a riot. All of a sudden, I was sure I knew why he had gotten his head chopped off.

I also was worried that all the laughing would bring my parents down. Somehow I didn't want to try to explain to them what a fifth century idiot was doing in my basement after midnight.

"Look, Attila," I said, "can you . . . uh . . . move about? Go from place to place?"

"Why not?" the Hun said.

"Well, I want you to come with me," I said. "I want you to meet this guy, Lamont Penumbra, the one who summoned you. He'll be very happy to see that his spell worked."

"Spell!" Attila said. "Railroad crossing: Look out for the cars—Can you spell it without any 'r's?"

"I—T," I said.

"Oh," Attila said.

"Now, look," I told the Hunnish clown, "we have to climb out this window. I'm going to turn out the lights so my parents will think I'm asleep."

"Lights!" Attila said. "Do you know how many Visigoths it takes to screw in a new candle?"

"Tell me later," I said and pushed the giggling ghost out the window up onto the sidewalk.

11

Getting Attila through the streets of Hoboken was something of a problem. He kept wanting to stop and look at things and tell stale jokes. For example, he went into a bar and said, "Hey! Do you serve spirits here?"

Apparently everybody could see him, not just me. He didn't look particularly ghostly, just messy and dirty.

I knew where to find Steve and Lamont Penumbra. They would be at Kevin Schwartz's Pizzeria. It was Steve's favorite place, and he often went there for three or four pizzas after closing the Magic Moscow.

When we got to the pizzeria, I could see Steve and Lamont Penumbra through the window. They were sharing Kevin Schwartz's super special thirty-six-inch pizza. I dragged Attila into the restaurant.

"Hey!" he said. "An Italian restaurant! Do they serve spookghetti here?"

"Steve," I said, "we've got a problem."

Lamont Penumbra almost choked on his pizza when I told him who Attila was. At first he didn't believe me. He thought that Attila was just some weirdo, and that I was trying to play a joke on him. As I said, Attila didn't look much like a ghost—at least not anybody's idea of a ghost. Finally, they began to believe me, because, as Steve said, it would be hard for anyone to get to be as dirty as Attila in less than fifteen hundred years.

When it finally sank in that this was a ghost of an almost famous person from history and that the spell had actually worked, Lamont Penumbra was so happy that he sort of went crazy.

"It worked! It worked! The spell worked!" he shouted. Lamont Penumbra got up and started capering around.

"Take it easy!" Steve said. "Don't lose your head."

That was the wrong thing to say. "I can take my head off," Attila said. "Want to see?"

"NO!" we all shouted.

It turned out that ghosts don't actually eat, but they enjoy sniffing food. After we got Lamont Penumbra somewhat calmed down, we ordered a second super special thirty-six-inch pizza for Attila to inhale over. He liked it very much and said that pizza had been improved a lot since his day.

Attila caused a certain amount of stir in the pizzeria; not because he was a ghost—only we knew that—but because he was so weird looking. Fortunately, Kevin Schwartz is a good guy, or he might have asked us to leave.

Steve was very impressed to be sitting at a table with Attila the Pun. "I always liked your brother, the Hun," he said.

"Sure," Attila said. "Everybody likes him—but it's not true that he had a great sense of humor. You probably heard that he did, didn't you?"

"Mostly I heard that he rode around on a shaggy pony and everybody was afraid of him," Steve said.

"Well, that part is true," Attila the Pun said, "but any jokes you may have heard that he supposedly told were probably mine. For example, there's this famous one: How do you find your dog if he's lost in the woods?"

None of us knew.

"You put your ear to a tree and listen to the bark," Attila the Pun said. "Now that's one that everybody claims was told by my brother, the Hun—but it's my joke. I've been very ill-treated by history."

"That's a shame," Lamont Penumbra said.

"It is," Attila said, "and the rotten part of it is, when you're dead, you can't do anything about it. Live people can say or write anything, and you just have to put up with it. That's why I'm not so famous, and my brother is."

"What's it like, being dead?" I asked.

"Oh, it's nice," Attila said, "but it gets boring after a few hundred years. I'm glad you summoned me. If you're not going to finish that root beer, I'd like to sniff it."

"I guess things were very different when you were alive," Steve said.

"I'll say," Attila said. "I traveled all over with my brother, and I never came across pizza like this. I wish I could eat it. You guys are living at the right time, that's for sure."

It was interesting, sitting around with a ghost from the fifth century. Of course, it was hard to get Attila to tell us things about when he was alive. Mostly he wanted to tell jokes. I was surprised to learn that all the elephant jokes the kids tell in school were already popular back then.

About the time Attila was telling his fiftieth elephant joke—the one that goes, "How do you know if there's an elephant in your tent?"—I started yawning.

"Say, it's pretty late," Steve said. "Norman, you'd better go home and get some sleep."

"Okay," Attila said. "Let's go, Norman."

"Wait a minute," I said. "Is he going to come home with me?"

"Of course," Attila said, "I have to stay with you. You're the one who summoned me."

"I keep telling you," I said, "it was really Lamont Penumbra who summoned you. I think you ought to go to his place." I just didn't want to have to deal with explaining Attila to my parents. They'd given me enough trouble about the moose head—and Attila really *did* have fleas.

"Well, if you say so," Attila said.

"Uh, do you . . . do ghosts . . . sleep, or what?" Lamont Penumbra asked.

"No, ghosts don't sleep," Attila said. "Mostly, I pace up and down and talk to myself; I sing Hunnish songs and whack things with my sword all night. But you go ahead and sleep. I'll be fine by myself."

"Right," I said, "I'll be going now."

"Me, too," Steve said. "Let's all meet for breakfast at the Magic Moscow."

"Fair enough," Attila said, "I'll go with Lamont. By the way, do you know the difference between a rain cloud and an Ostrogoth with his toe cut off?"

Nobody said anything. It was maybe the two-hundredth riddle of the evening.

"One pours with rain, and the other roars with pain," Attila said.

"Good night, Attila," I said.

"Good night, Attila," Steve said.

"Good night! Don't let the bedbugs bite!" Attila said.

12

I usually eat breakfast at the Magic Moscow during the summer. Steve doesn't serve breakfast to the public. The Magic Moscow opens at lunchtime. My mother hates to cook breakfast, so she's happy that I get fed at work. I like to eat there because Steve is very good at experimental breakfasts. For example, he makes scrambled eggs with chili peppers, toasted carrot cereal, and avocado pancakes—none of which I ever get at home.

On the morning following Attila's appearance, I arrived at the Magic Moscow bright and early. Lamont Penumbra was already there, having a coffee omelet. It was the first time I had ever seen Lamont Penumbra outside his loft without his black hat and coat. He was wearing a pair of blue jeans and a T-shirt with the three little pigs on it. He looked as if he hadn't had much sleep.

"Hi, Norman," he said. "I haven't had much sleep."

"Eat your eggs," Steve said. "They're full of caffeine."

Attila was wandering around behind the counter, sniffing his breakfast. "Hey!" he said to me. "This is a soda fountain! You work here—do you know how to make an elephant float?"

"Tie little water wings on him?" I asked.

"No," Attila said. "To make an elephant float, you need two scoops of ice cream, some root beer, an elephant, and a really huge blender."

"So how's everything?" I asked Lamont Penumbra, sitting down at the table. Steve went behind the counter to make me a bean-sprout omelet, my current favorite.

"That ghost is murder," Lamont Penumbra said. "All night he was stomping up and down, singing horrible songs in Hun, or whatever his native language is. And he told jokes to himself, and he laughed at them. I counted four hundred and fifty elephant jokes before I finally fell asleep from sheer exhaustion. And he whacked stuff with his sword. He whacked most of the stuffing out of my sofa. I can't stand another night with him in my place. What's more, I keep scratching. Is it possible to catch fleas from a ghost?"

"It's hard to string a violin," Attila said. "It takes guts." Then he stuck his nose up the spout of the soft ice-cream machine.

Steve brought me my bean-sprout omelet. "That Attila's a real problem," he said. "The only one who likes him without any reservations is Edward."

Edward, the Malamute dog, had taken a great fancy to the Hunnish slob and was following him everywhere, with his tail wagging.

"It's not that Attila isn't a nice fellow in an ancient, moronic sort of way—it's just that he's very hard to have around," Steve whispered.

"So what we wanted to know, Norman . . ." Lamont Penumbra whispered.

". . . is, what are you going to do with him?" Steve continued.

"Me?" I asked, astonished. "Why me? What's this got to do with me?"

"Well, Attila thinks you're responsible for him," Steve said.

"He says that no matter who started the spell, you were the one who summoned him," Lamont Penumbra said.

"He says he's your responsibility, and you have to decide what to do with him," Steve said. "We all discussed it before breakfast."

"Thanks a lot," I said. "I'm just a kid, and you guys are trying to fob off the responsibility for a Hun who's been dead for fifteen hundred years on me. That's really nice."

"Norman, it's just that he's making me crazy," Lamont Penumbra said.

"He says he doesn't have to listen to us," Steve said. "He says you're the only mortal he has to take any account of."

"Talk to him," Lamont Penumbra said. "Tell him he can't stay in my loft any more."

Just then, Bruce the Milkman arrived.

"Hey! A milkman!" Attila said. "What has only one horn and gives milk? Give up? A milk truck!"

"Who's this guy?" Bruce asked. "He looks like Attila the Hun."

"Typical," Attila said. "Say, milkman, why does the ocean roar?"

"I don't know," Bruce the Milkman said. "Why *does* the ocean roar?"

"You'd roar too if you had crabs on your bottom," Attila said.

"Say, this guy's pretty funny," Bruce the Milkman said. "Is he going to be performing here all the time?" Bruce carried the last of the empties out to his wagon, clucked to his horse, Cheryl, and drove off.

"Talk to him," Steve whispered.

"Um . . . Attila," I said.

"Right. . . . Did you see that guy's horse? How many legs does a horse have?"

"Four," I said.

"Wrong! Six! Forelegs in front and two in back."

"Attila, how long are you planning to stay?" I asked.

"How long?"

"Yes," I said, "I mean, don't you have things to do? Don't you have to get back to being . . . uh . . . dead?"

"Not really," Attila said. "Don't you worry, I can stay for a long time."

"Uh . . . you don't want to go back to being . . ."

"Dead? No, I like it here. I'm going to sniff some more of that pizza tonight."

Attila went into the storeroom to sniff the jars of cherries in Red Dye Number Two that Steve kept there. I went back to the table where Steve and Lamont Penumbra were sitting.

"He says he likes it here," I said. "He says he likes the way the food smells. He says he doesn't have to go back for a long time."

"What are we going to do with him?" Lamont Penumbra said. "He's not staying at my place anymore, that's final."

"Lamont, isn't there a spell for sending him back where he came from?"

"You think I didn't look that up at three this morning?" Lamont Penumbra asked. "Of course there's a spell, but the ghost has to be willing to go. You see, it works like this. Most ghosts want to go back. They like it there. When you're a ghost, you sort of stay in a time and place comparable to where you were when you were alive. So Attila doesn't feel like going back to what must be a bunch of fifth-century Huns, where the pizza isn't any good. Sooner or later he'll go back by himself or I can cast a spell and send him—but until then, he's with us."

Attila came out of the storeroom. "You know what you get if you cross a cat and a lemon?" he asked. "A sourpuss!"

13

I t was up to me to figure out what to do with Attila. Steve and Lamont Penumbra didn't seem to have any ideas. Attila probably never had an idea in his life—or after.

I went and got a chocolate-dipped frozen carrot from the freezer and munched it while I thought things over. Meanwhile, Steve and Lamont Penumbra sat around, looking bewildered, and Attila sniffed this and that and occasionally told a joke.

Then it came to me! A great idea! If it worked, it would be one of the great ideas of all time.

"Look, Steve," I said, "you always worry that someone will break into the Magic Moscow at night and maybe steal Edward, right?"

"Well, yes," Steve said. "Edward is a valuable dog—and most of my comics are here, too. I was thinking that maybe I should get a burglar alarm."

"How about something better than a burglar alarm?" I said. "How about a real live—or in this case, a real dead—night watchman?"

"You mean Attila?" Lamont Penumbra asked. "It won't work. Attila doesn't like to be alone."

"He wouldn't be alone," I said. "Edward would be with him. Edward likes him."

"That's because Edward doesn't understand his jokes," Lamont Penumbra said.

"It might be all right," Steve said.

"Of course it will," I said. "Attila doesn't eat food—he only sniffs it—so it won't cost anything to keep him."

"But during the day, Attila will drive the customers crazy by telling jokes," Steve said. "How will we get him to agree to sort of stay out of sight during business hours?"

"I've thought of that, too," I said. "If Attila agrees, I think there's a way to keep him happy, and everybody else, too. Will you give my idea a try?"

"Sure," Steve said, "it's the only idea we've got."

"Okay," I said, "I'm going to have a talk with Attila now, and if he agrees, we'll give my idea a try."

14

A ttila agreed. I got busy making posters and putting them up all over Hoboken.

The posters invited everyone in town to come to the Magic Moscow that night for free toasted carrot sandwiches and goat's milk malteds and to hear a concert of recorded jazz music and a surprise "live" entertainer.

The entertainer was Attila, of course. He spent the whole day in the storeroom, practicing his material—as if he hadn't had enough practice in fifteen hundred years. We closed the Magic Moscow for an hour after the suppertime rush and arranged all the chairs and tables so the people would be able to see the stage. The stage was a space in front of the counter lit by a spotlight I got from my room—something I had found in the street and repaired.

It was a Friday night, and we got a pretty good crowd. In fact, the place was just about full. Steve had added a black clip-on bow tie to the white soda jerk uniform he always wore. He stood at the door and shook hands with everybody as they came in. Lamont Penumbra and I served the toasted carrot sandwiches and goat's milk malteds, and we changed the records on Steve's record player. He had selected a bunch of boogie-woogie piano records for the evening, and the people at the tables were tapping their feet and having a good time.

Then, we turned down the lights and switched on the spotlight. Steve stepped into the circle of light and said, "Ladies and gentlemen, the Magic Moscow is proud to present a great comedian, the late Attila the Pun!"

Attila came out of the storeroom. He was sweating. "Good evening, ladies and germs," he said. "Did you hear about the two cannonballs? They got married and had B.B.'s!"

The audience laughed.

"Hey! I'm a ghost, you know?" Attila said. He was getting comfortable. "You know what ghosts eat for breakfast? Ghost toasties! Hey! Do you know what ghosts like to do at the amusement park? They ride the roller ghoster! Hey! Are you all enjoying your ghost milk malteds? Hey! You know what a spirit on guard duty says? Who ghost there? Hey!"

The audience loved him. It turned out that fifth-century Hun humor really goes over well in Hoboken. Attila told jokes for almost an hour. Finally Steve had to lead him off, saying, "Save something for next Friday night."

"I've got a million of them!" Attila said.

Attila's act at the Magic Moscow is the biggest thing in Hoboken. Some Friday nights we can hardly get all the people inside. Steve is happy because he doesn't have to worry about someone breaking in at night and stealing Edward, and he likes playing the old jazz records for the people who come to laugh at Attila's jokes.

Attila is happy. He was so grateful to me for thinking up my great idea that he is letting me keep his sword for him. It looks really good, Attila's genuine fifth-century Hun sword, hanging from the antlers of my stuffed moose.

Jolly Roger

A Dog of Hoboken

Jolly Roger was a real dog, and most of the story is true. Pretty much everything the dog does in the story really happened, including the things that happen to him and the way people feel about him. It's hardly fiction at all. At some point Jolly Roger went away, or maybe he died. The garage where he used to hang out closed, and the non-fictional guys who worked there weren't around much. Except one of them . . . and Jolly Roger's son, Jolly. Jolly looked a little like his father, not quite as large, and he worked at a small parking lot down the block from my house. Jolly knew all the tricks. His father had taught him how to gather newspapers and stuff them under a car to make a warm nest, and how to run the wrong way up a one-way street to escape the dog catcher's truck. Jolly was a smart dog.

He was the mortal enemy of my dog, Arnold. Arnold hated him. Arnold was a big Malamute (there are more Malamutes in another part of this book), and to be honest, he wasn't all that clever. Whenever Jolly saw Arnold he would do something, or say something, in some way dogs communicate that we don't know anything about. What Jolly would do or say was extremely insulting. Arnold would roar and lunge, and my wife, Jill, or I would have a hard time hanging onto the leash. While Arnold was roaring, Jolly would scamper off, feeling pleased with himself.

We had another Malamute, Juno, who was more or less normal, and couldn't have cared less about Arnold's feud with Jolly. Juno and Arnold and Jill and I dealt with it by always going the other way along the block when it was daytime, when Jolly would be at the parking lot. At night

Jolly would go home with his boss, and we could take walks past the lot, in the direction of the Erie Lackawanna railroad station.

One night I had gone into the station and gotten two cups of coffee at the stand there. I brought them to Jill, who was waiting near the statue of Sam Sloan. I didn't actually know who Sam Sloan was—I suppose he had something to do with the Erie Lackawanna Railroad. Jill was holding Arnold's leash. I was holding Juno's leash and balancing two Styrofoam cups of coffee. I handed one to Jill.

Then, she vanished. Vanished into thin air. She just disappeared from sight. In an instant. I saw the Styrofoam cup of coffee suspended for what seemed like seconds in mid-air. It was like some kind of magic.

Here's how the magic trick happened: Not far from the statue of Sam Sloan was Duke's House, an old-fashioned saloon. It had those swinging doors, such as you see in cowboy movies. Double swinging doors that don't come as high as your head, and don't come very close to the ground. If you were a dog, you'd be able to see under the doors and into the saloon. Arnold could see, and what he saw was . . . Jolly!

What the people drinking in the bar saw was a big dog—with a leash attached, and attached to the leash a surprised red-headed woman being dragged along the ground—streak under the swinging doors and rush at a dog . . . not Jolly . . . Jolly's brother.

I have to give Arnold credit for realizing, when he got close, that the dog was not his mortal enemy, and not carrying out his plan to kill him . . . if he'd ever had a plan. Everything was explained to the people in the saloon, and Jill became even more popular in the neighborhood.

1

J olly Roger came to Hoboken on a ship from Alaska, the *Matilda Magoo*. It was named for the captain's sister. The captain was Matthew Magoo, and he was a good captain too. The only thing wrong with Captain Magoo was that he was too softhearted. He would allow little privileges to the men in his crew, and little favors, and permission to do this and that, and soon things would get out of hand. For example, there was the matter of pets. First a sailor came on board with a little gray kitten. The sailor's name was Norway Ned.

"Oh, please, please, please, Captain Magoo, let me keep the kitten!" Norway Ned had said. Captain Magoo told Norway Ned he could keep the kitten as long as he remembered to feed it and didn't let the kitten make a mess of things aboard ship.

The kitten named Mitten was a great favorite of the sailors, and when the *Matilda Magoo* came into port again, a sailor named Jutland Jed came aboard with a kitten of his own, a black one named Nitten.

"You allowed Norway Ned to have a kitten," Jutland Jed said to Captain Magoo. "I've been on this ship twice as long as Norway Ned, so I should be allowed to have a kitten too."

Of course, there was nothing for Captain Magoo to do except allow Jutland Jed to keep his kitten named Nitten.

At the next port a sailor named Fiji Fred brought five kittens aboard—never mind what their names were. He went to see Captain Magoo.

"I work five times as hard as Norway Ned and Jutland Jed," Fiji Fred said. "So I should be allowed to keep my five kittens, never mind what their names are."

What could Captain Magoo do but say yes?

It wasn't long before the ship became a sort of floating zoo. The crew had kittens and cats, dogs and parrots, rats and mice, monkeys, fish, snakes, and even spiders.

Captain Magoo got fed up. "This is what comes of my being nice to Norway Ned!" he said. "I'm going to put my foot down! The next port we strike, every animal goes off this ship. I mean it!"

The next port for the *Matilda Magoo* was Hoboken. Captain Magoo told the crew they had forty-eight hours to sell, trade, or give away their animals. The sailors were unhappy about the orders, but a sailor always obeys his captain, so they trooped into town to sell, trade, and give away their pets.

At the end of two days the crew of the *Matilda Magoo* had sold, swapped, and made presents of cats and dogs and mice and parrots and any number of animals—all except a puppy belonging to a sailor named Texas Ted. This puppy was Texas Ted's pride and joy. It was half Chinese Chow Chow, and half Alaskan Husky. Its name was Jolly Roger.

Texas Ted just couldn't find anyone to give his puppy to. The fact is, he didn't want to give his puppy to anyone, and he didn't look very hard. He hoped that somehow Captain Magoo would change his mind and let him keep Jolly Roger. Texas Ted was the oldest and toughest sailor on the *Matilda Magoo*. He didn't really believe that the captain would force him to give up his Chow Chow Husky puppy. When the time came to sail, Captain Magoo gave Texas Ted his orders: "As captain of this vessel, I order you to put that pooch ashore, period."

Texas Ted was rough and tough, but he was a good sailor, and he knew that orders are orders. He carried Jolly Roger down the gangplank, and looked around for someone to give him to. "Tie him to that post," Captain Magoo said, "and let's get underway!"

Texas Ted couldn't do that—but the *Matilda Magoo* was about to weigh anchor—and Ted knew he must do his duty. Just then, The Kid came along. The Kid was a Hoboken kid. He earned his living parking cars in a parking lot. "Hey, Kid," Texas Ted said. "You want this puppy?"

And that is how Jolly Roger came to Hoboken.

2

The Kid had a job in a parking garage in Hoboken, and that's where he took Jolly Roger. The Kid's boss was called Marvin the Ape.

"Hey Kid, you're twelve minutes late," Marvin the Ape said. "You want I should fire you and maybe jump up and down on your head?"

"Hey, don't hit me Boss!" The Kid said. "Look, I got this puppy!"

"Awww, he's cute," Marvin the Ape said. "What's his name?"

"His name is Jolly Roger, Boss. He came off a ship from Alaska. He's part Chinese Chow Chow, and part Alaskan Husky. His father was the toughest dog in Fairbanks. A sailor gave him to me."

"Well, get to work, or I'll tie knots in your arms and legs—and that would upset the puppy. Kootchie-koo, little Jolly Roger," Marvin the Ape said.

The Kid's job was to wash cars, and wax cars, and park cars for people when they brought them into the garage, and to go and get the cars for those people when they came back. Every day The Kid would take Jolly Roger to work. Every day Marvin the Ape would shout threats at The Kid and secretly give cookies to Jolly Roger.

Jolly Roger had his own doghouse inside the garage, near the place where The Kid washed cars. Washing cars was Jolly Roger's favorite activity at the garage.

In those days Jolly Roger liked everybody, and played with all the people who came to the garage—like any puppy. But Alaskan Huskies in general, and Chinese Chow Chows in particular, are not the sort of dogs to play with just anyone. Alaskan Huskies and Chinese Chow Chows are both very particular breeds. They have their dignity. As Jolly Roger grew up he stopped romping with people— and he did not allow people to pet him.

The only exception was The Kid. The Kid could throw a ball for Jolly Roger to chase, and wrestle with Jolly Roger, and get Jolly Roger to lie on his back and wave all four paws in the air.

It bothered Marvin the Ape. "How come The Kid is the only person Jolly Roger wants to play with?" he asked. "I have been giving him cookies for a year."

That's the way it sometimes is with Alaskan Huskies and Chinese Chow Chows.

3

Ordinarily, it is not such a good idea to let dogs roam around loose, especially in a busy place like Hoboken—but in Jolly Roger's case there was no choice. The Kid had nothing to say about it. One day Jolly Roger disappeared around the corner and was gone for three hours.

The Kid was worried about Jolly Roger but Marvin the Ape said, "Listen—dogs will be dogs. You've got to let Jolly Roger go around by himself or the other dogs will think he's a weenie."

It was good advice. It was also notable that Marvin the Ape did not threaten The Kid.

When Jolly Roger came back he looked worn out. He also was covered with mud, and he appeared to have been chewed on. He was tired. He was thirsty. He drank a great deal of water. Jolly Roger was obviously very happy. The Kid got the hose, the one he washed cars with, and gave Jolly Roger a bath.

"I guess Jolly Roger found some other dogs to play with," Marvin the Ape said. "By the way, you don't expect to use my water for free, do you?"

After the first time, Jolly Roger went off by himself every day—and he stayed away longer every time. The Kid tried tying Jolly Roger up, but the Chow Chow Husky cried and whined and chewed at the rope until

The Kid let him go. Sometimes Jolly Roger would be gone all day.

The Kid began spending his lunch hour wandering around Hoboken looking for Jolly Roger. He found him. Jolly Roger was spending time with the dock dogs. The dock dogs were the rough, tough dogs of the Hoboken waterfront. For blocks along River Street there was a big iron fence. Behind the fence were docks where ships came to load and unload. The area behind the fence belonged to the rough tough longshoremen who did the loading and unloading, and to the rough tough dock dogs. Jolly Roger had made friends with both the longshoremen and the dogs.

These dogs were three-quarters wild. No one could touch them. They ran and played and fought behind the iron fence. The longshoremen shared their lunches with the dogs and chased away the Hoboken dog catcher whenever he came. At night the wild Hoboken dock dogs ran through the streets of the waterfront neighborhood, knocking over garbage cans, barking, and lunging at cats. These were the dogs that adopted Jolly Roger, the young dog from Alaska.

4

The leader of the dock dogs was a big black dog. Some of the longshoremen called him Brutus MacDougal Bugleboy. He was some tough dog. Some said Brutus MacDougal Bugleboy was part Labrador Retriever, some said he was part Newfoundland dog. Most people said and believed that he was part African Upland Gorilla.

Brutus MacDougal Bugleboy had a nasty temper. The Hoboken dock dogs knew it. The rough tough longshoremen knew it. More than once a big strong longshoreman, who carried 200 pound bags of coffee beans on his shoulder, had to be rescued from the top of a big crate by other longshoremen because Brutus MacDougal Bugleboy had taken a sudden dislike to him. If Brutus MacDougal Bugleboy liked someone he would just ignore that person.

It was Brutus MacDougal Bugleboy that Jolly Roger had his fight with. It didn't happen right away. At first, when Jolly Roger began hanging out with the wild Hoboken dock dogs, he was little more than a puppy. Jolly Roger was polite to every one of the dock dogs. They, in turn, teased him, and chased him, and took special pleasure in rolling him in the mud until he looked like a giant dirtball, but no dog ever hurt him. Except Brutus MacDougal Bugleboy. Brutus bit Jolly Roger, painfully, right on the nose. Brutus MacDougal Bugleboy did that to every new dog in the pack. It was his favorite trick. It was Brutus MacDougal Bugleboy's intention that the new dog remember the bite, and remember to be afraid of Brutus.

Jolly Roger remembered the bite, but he also remembered that he had not had a chance to bite Brutus MacDougal Bugleboy on *his* nose. Jolly Roger planned to do that. In fact, Jolly Roger planned to chase Brutus MacDougal Bugleboy away, and become leader of the dock dogs himself—just like that. Some dogs are dominant. (That means they *have* to run things.) Jolly Roger was a dominant dog. Either he would be the boss of the Hoboken dock dogs, or he would leave the docks forever and live off scraps in alleys in the back of town. Jolly Roger did not expect to lose the fight. It would be Brutus MacDougal Bugleboy who would live on handouts in the alley.

And that is exactly what happened. Those who saw the fight said it was not much. Jolly Roger walked up to Brutus MacDougal Bugleboy one day and bit him, very hard, on the nose. There was some scuffling and growling, and Brutus MacDougal Bugleboy took off for the back of town. He was never seen on the waterfront again. Brutus knew that Jolly Roger was the better dog, and he didn't stay around to find out just how much better.

Jolly Roger didn't have a scratch on him. He looked around, offering to fight any other dog that was interested. No dogs were interested. Then the wild Hoboken dog pack settled back into its normal routine, with one exception: Jolly Roger was king of the waterfront.

5

Jolly Roger started staying out all night. Sometimes The Kid would not see his dog for two or three days. Jolly Roger was an important citizen. As king of the waterfront, Jolly Roger had many things to do. First of all, he had to receive the respect of all the other dogs. There were the regular dock dogs, strangers passing through, and house pets who would run away and join the dock dogs for a day and then go home. Some dogs were let out each morning by their owners to spend the day on the waterfront, and at night they would go home. One man drove in each day from another town with two pedigreed hunting dogs. The hunting dogs would spend the day on the docks while their master worked, and go home with him at night.

All these dogs had to go and see Jolly Roger every day. Jolly Roger would lie in the patch of grass behind the big iron fence in the morning, and each dog would slink up to him with its head held sideways, and put its muzzle under Jolly Roger's chin, or sniff his whiskers. This is a way dogs have of showing respect. Jolly Roger would give a little sniff to each dog to let it know he had accepted its greeting. Sometimes there would be twenty or thirty dogs taking part in this ceremony.

Jolly Roger decided which dogs would be allowed to stay with the pack, and which would be chased away. He broke up fights, and protected young and small dogs. He never bit any dog on the nose as Brutus had done—and he got into very few fights. Most dogs decided from the look of Jolly Roger that they didn't want to fight with him.

Jolly Roger got first sniff at any food the longshoremen offered the dock dogs. If Jolly Roger didn't like the smell of it, and didn't eat any, neither did the other dogs.

Jolly Roger decided who the pack should be afraid of and who they should and should not like. Many of the dock dogs had never been touched by a human, and they were afraid of them. Jolly Roger was comfortable with people and understood them—so the dock dogs depended on his judgment of the humans they met.

Jolly Roger protected mother dogs and new puppies. The puppies all looked like him. He picked out safe, secret places for the puppies to be hidden, and helped to guard them.

When the weather began to grow cold, Jolly Roger would show the younger dogs how to sweep newspaper and leaves together under parked cars and against walls to make warm nests to sleep in.

The most important thing Jolly Roger did was to teach the other dogs how to keep away from the Hoboken municipal dog catcher. The dog catcher drove around in a little truck. His dearest wish was to catch every one of the Hoboken dock dogs. One trick Jolly Roger taught the dock dogs was to run the wrong way up a one-way street when the dog catcher was after them in his truck.

Sometimes Jolly Roger would let himself be caught so the others could get away. Jolly Roger had been caught lots of times. There would always be someone watching who would go and tell The Kid. The Kid would go to the dog pound and pay a fine, and get Jolly Roger out. A number of times The Kid was not needed. Jolly Roger had broken away from the dog catcher 7 times, had broken out of the dog catcher's truck 9 times, and had broken out of the dog pound 5 times—a total of 21 escapes.

Even though The Kid didn't see Jolly Roger every day, Jolly Roger was still his dog. Jolly Roger was not The Kid's dog because The Kid took Jolly Roger home with him, and he was not The Kid's dog because The Kid fed him— because The Kid didn't do those things very often once Jolly Roger was king of the waterfront. He was not even The Kid's dog because The Kid would go down to the dog pound to pay Jolly Roger's fine when he got caught. Jolly Roger was The Kid's dog because The Kid was the only person Jolly Roger would allow to pet him, and The Kid was the only person who could get Jolly Roger to play, and The Kid was the only person who could get Jolly Roger to lie on his back and wave all four paws in the air.

6

While Jolly Roger was clearly The Kid's dog and nobody else's, he also had a great many friends, human and animal. At times, Jolly Roger would disappear from the waterfront. People would report seeing him a mile away at the other end of Hoboken, or two or three miles away in the next town.

"I saw Jolly Roger way up in Weehawken," someone might say.

"Jolly Roger was having a hamburger over in Jersey City this morning," someone else might say.

Every afternoon, during his break, the cook from the Five Star Chinese-American Restaurant would appear at the iron fence, carrying two big plates of shrimp egg foo yung, Jolly Roger's favorite.

The cops especially liked Jolly Roger, and nearly every time the dog catcher got him, they would arrest the dog catcher and throw him in jail for a few hours.

And there was a millionaire who parked his car at the garage five days a week. Sometimes, on a Friday, the millionaire would invite Jolly Roger to get into his car, which was a big and fancy one. Jolly Roger would hop in, and sit on the front seat. The millionaire would take Jolly Roger to his estate in the country, and entertain him for the weekend. When Jolly Roger would come back on Monday, he would burp a good deal, and hardly touch his egg foo yung.

7

Once there was a big storm with high winds. Jolly Roger was sitting on the end of the pier, where the Erie Lakawanna tugboats tie up, looking into the distance and thinking. A really powerful gust of wind lifted Jolly Roger right off the pier and into the river ten feet below.

The river was whipped by the wind, and the current was strong. Jolly Roger was carried out into the channel, where he was certainly drowned. People saw this happen, but there was no chance of saving Jolly Roger. It all happened too fast. They told The Kid, who felt very bad. Everyone on the waterfront felt bad. They hated to think that they would never see Jolly Roger again.

Three days later, Jolly Roger crawled out of a storm sewer which connected with the river. He was very tired, and soaking wet. He slept all day at the garage. The Kid brought him bowls of hot soup whenever he woke up. The next morning he went back to the docks.

Once, in the middle of winter, Jolly Roger was sitting on the frozen edge of the river, when the piece of ice he was sitting on broke off. Jolly Roger, still sitting calmly, floated out into the middle of the river and began moving into New York Harbor. He was in mid-river, heading for the Statue of Liberty when he was sighted by the crew of one of the Erie Lakawanna tugs. They called to him, and he hopped off the ice, swam to the tug, was taken aboard, and brought back to Hoboken wrapped in a towel. Jolly Roger had five sardine sandwiches prepared by the cook on the tug boat. He appeared to have enjoyed the experience.

8

S ome men came to see Marvin the Ape.

"We thought we would tear down your garage, and build a Turkish bath," the men said. "Of course, if you don't want to sell it to us, we could tap lumps on your head for two or three hours while you think it over."

"As a matter of fact," Marvin the Ape said, "I have been thinking about getting into the potato chip business down in Florida."

"Fine," the men said. "Here's the money. Get lost."

"Kid, you want to go to Florida and get rich in the potato chip game?" Marvin the Ape asked The Kid.

"I guess so," The Kid said. The Kid was thinking about how hard it would be to leave Jolly Roger.

"Get your stuff together, bean-head," Marvin the Ape said. "We'll leave for Florida tomorrow."

The Kid wandered out into the alley. He was thinking about his dog, Jolly Roger, the king of the waterfront. Jolly Roger had been king of the waterfront for a long time—longer than any other dog had ever been. Sooner or later, Jolly Roger would have to retire—but then he would probably go to live with his millionaire friend in the country, or retire to a warm corner of the Five Star Chinese-American Restaurant. He wouldn't want to go to Florida with The Kid and Marvin the Ape to be in the potato chip business.

Just then, Jolly Roger himself turned up. The Kid noticed that Jolly Roger had gotten sort of gray around the muzzle. Jolly Roger wagged his tail, and made a few playful jumps of the sort he never let anyone see but The Kid.

The Kid scratched Jolly Roger's head and told him all about how he had to go to Florida to be in the potato chip business. He told Jolly Roger how much he'd miss him. He told him goodbye.

The next morning, The Kid loaded his stuff into Marvin the Ape's big, shiny car. They were going to drive straight through to Florida, non-stop. The Kid took a last look at Hoboken before getting into the car. Marvin the Ape started the engine. The Kid shut the door. The car started rolling.

Just then The Kid and Marvin the Ape heard furious barking. It was Jolly Roger running at top speed after the car. Marvin the Ape stopped the car. The Kid opened the door. Jolly Roger jumped into the car, and settled down on the front seat between The Kid and Marvin the Ape.

"Jolly! Do you want to come to Florida with us, and be in the potato chip business?" The Kid asked.

"Woof woof woof woof!" Jolly Roger barked.

"You're going to retire from being king of the water-front?"

"Woof woof woof woof!" Jolly Roger said.

"I guess he's coming with us," The Kid said.

"I guess so," Marvin the Ape said. He stepped on the gas, and the big car started moving toward the Jersey Turnpike.

LOOKING FOR BOBOWICZ

Another story that is part of a trilogy. The first is a sort of almost famous book, The Hoboken Chicken Emergency, *which I guess you could say is a classic . . . stupid classic. The third book in this trilogy is* The Artsy Smartsy Club. *What these books have in common is a giant chicken. Very few authors can make that statement. Reading this story is educational. There are several actual historical facts. Please do not skip reading it because I told you that.*

1

On Friday I had my last day at Happy Valley Elementary School. On Saturday the moving truck came and took all our stuff to Hoboken, New Jersey and we left our house in Happy Valley forever. On Sunday our first day in the new house, the temperature was one hundred degrees Fahrenheit—the beginning of the hottest heat wave ever recorded in Hoboken in the month of June for 120 years.

One hundred and twenty years ago was when our Hoboken house had been built. This is what my parents did. They gave up a modern house in Happy Valley New Jersey—a house with a front yard, a backyard, and trees, on a street with similar houses and similar trees—to move to a brick house with no front yard, practically no backyard, and no trees, on a street with guys sitting on the steps drinking cans of beer and spitting on the sidewalk, and cars and buses running right past our door. And the Hoboken house was in rotten condition and cost three times as much as we got for our Happy Valley house.

My parents said we were going to fix up the house and have an "urban lifestyle." This is what an urban lifestyle is: My bike was stolen the first hour we were in town. And it was one hundred degrees Fahrenheit. My mother said she didn't want me growing up in a suburb. She said life was real in cities. I went upstairs to sit in my crummy 120-year-old room.

2

My father climbed the stairs to my room.

"Egad! It's hot as an oven in here, old pal," he said.

My father says things like "egad" and "odds bodkin." They have no meaning. I simply tolerate these weirdnesses, along with so many things my parents do.

"Sorry about your bike, old man," my father said.

He calls me *old man*, also *old chap.* There is no explanation for this.

"We'll get you another bike, I promise," he said. "But could you possibly wait until your birthday? There are a lot of expenses fixing up the new house."

This was great. I could have a bike for my birthday, instead of some other present, which I would have gotten if I was not to get a bike, which I would not be getting if the one I already had hadn't been stolen, which it probably would not have been if we had not moved to Hoboken, which was not my idea in the first place.

Okay, it wasn't a great bike. My mother had gotten it for me at a garage sale. It was one of those shorty models, for little kids—not the on-purpose low-slung kind with the banana seat and the fake roll bar. Those too are uncool, but this was just like a shrunken normal bike. And it was a girl's bike. It was light blue with pink hearts and flowers painted on the frame. I had removed the white wicker basket with plastic flowers, but it still looked girly. Also the front wheel had a bad wiggle, and the brakes didn't really work. So it was an awful bike—it was still mine—it was transportation—and somebody had stolen it—and it wasn't my idea to move to Hoboken—and it wasn't a very nice thing to happen to me right away on my first day.

"That will be fine, Dad," I said.

"Good show, old man," my father said. "Now about this room . . . I don't see how you can stand it. Maybe you'd like us to drag your mattress into our room, where it's nice and cool."

My parents' bedroom had a little dinky air conditioner that puffed air about three degrees cooler than what was outside. It was pathetic.

"I'll be fine here, Dad," I said.

"Good lad. Now do you want to help us scrape paint off the woodwork or just explore around?"

"I think I'll do some exploring," I said.

3

I had already had a quick look at the basement, and I wanted to go back. It was huge! It went on forever. It was very deep, which gave it a high ceiling, and it was full of wonderful junk!

The house may have been 120 years old, but at least two hundred years' worth of stuff was piled up in the basement. Things were piled up so that you couldn't make out separate objects all at once. At first it looked like a giant tangle, and then, in the light of the bare lightbulbs, you'd start to see individual things, one at a time.

There was a workbench, covered with dust, and a few rusty tools. There were boxes and cartons and crates and coffee cans full of screws and nails. There was a bumper off a car, about fifteen busted tennis racquets, a stack of old-time TV sets piled one on top of another, a coil of wire that was as thick as my finger, a stuffed swordfish with a busted beak, (that was going on the wall in my room, I decided right away). And then I saw it. The fan!

It was a big fan, four feet in diameter, on a metal stand, like a flagpole. It was much taller than me. I had never seen anything like it. I plugged it into the electrical box behind the workbench and threw the switch. There was a buzzing noise, then a grinding, and the big blades began to turn in their metal cage. The whole top of the thing turned left and right, and as it picked up speed, it blew gritty dust everywhere. It worked! But it needed help. I switched it off. And pulled the plug.

I found a pair of pliers and a screwdriver, also a can of oil and some rags. I was going to have to take the thing apart, clean and oil it, and then get it upstairs to my bedroom. There would be no way to take it up in one piece. The base on which it stood must have weighed fifty pounds. I would have to sort of roll it up the stairs, resting on every step. The idea was, once I got the pieces up to my bedroom, I would put it together and have a cool room in more ways than one.

It took the rest of the day. I was pretty tired and dirty and oily and sweaty when I got the thing upstairs and back together, but it was worth it. It had cleaned up beautifully, and I had squirted oil into the little oil holes in the motor and along the spindle. When I plugged it in and switched it on, it made a lovely humming noise and turned its huge head from side to side. I found I had to put a pile of books on each corner of my bed to keep the sheets from blowing off. After that it was cool sleeping for me, right through the muggy, mosquito-infested, Hoboken heatwave night.

4

In the morning the sun came up looking like a red-hot penny. You could tell it was going to be another scorching day, the kind where you can fry an egg on the sidewalk. I stepped out the front door, intending to maybe do some exploring, and the heat smacked me in the face. I stepped back into the house. My parents were getting ready to go to work in air-conditioned offices in New York City, across the river. I was on my own.

I thought it might be a good idea to rummage around in the basement some more. The fan had been a good find, and it looked as though there was a lot more interesting stuff piled up in the dark corners. Also it would be cool down there—anyway, cooler.

There were two naked lightbulbs that hung down on their wires. You turned them on by pulling a string. Until you got to the first lightbulb, you had to make your way by the light that shone down the basement steps. It was a little scary and a little dangerous.

As I got to the bottom of the steps, and before I pulled the string on the first light, I thought I saw a dim blue-green glow coming from way back where it was darkest.

I stood and looked, opening my eyes as wide as I could. What could be making that light? When I turned the light on, I couldn't see it, and when I turned it off again, there it was. I tried to memorize the location and moved toward it, turning the lights on as I went.

I had to climb over some stuff—rusty bed-springs, broken furniture, things like that. Then I found the source of the greenish glow. There was a brick removed from the wall, up near the ceiling and way back in the basement. I stood on a little wooden barrel and was able to see that the brick behind had been removed, and the brick behind that, all the way through the wall and into the basement of the building next door. Obviously a pipe or something had once run between the buildings.

There was a light on in the other basement, and I could hear muffled voices and music. I don't know why I did this, but I put my mouth to the hole and hooted like an owl. "Whooo! Whooo!" The voices stopped.

"Whooo! Whooo!" The music stopped.

I thought I heard whispering.

Then I heard a voice come through the hole. "Is there somebody there?"

"I am Edmund Dantes," I said. "I have been unjustly imprisoned by my enemies." I got this from a Classics Comic of my father's—he saved them from his childhood and he lets me read them. This one was *The Count of Monte Cristo*. I'd like to read the actual book someday.

"I am the Abbe Faria," the voice said. "A priest, also unjustly imprisoned in the Chateau d'If."

That was incredible! The Abbe Faria is another character in the story. "How'd you know what I was talking about?" I asked into the hole.

"We've got about a hundred Classics Comics down here," the voice said. "You want to come over?"

5

I went next door. It was just like our house, only it was divided into apartments. It wasn't hard to find the door that led to the basement. There I found a boy and a girl, about my age. The boy would have been beautiful, if he were a girl. The girl would have been handsome, if she were a boy.

"Why is your hair like that?" the girl asked me.

"I sleep in front of a powerful fan," I said.

"My name is Loretta Fischetti," the girl said. "This is my friend Bruno Ugg. Bruno will not speak to you. He is not being rude. He took a vow of silence and can't speak to anyone. Bruno, when did you take the vow of silence?"

"Six o'clock yesterday. Rats! I talked! Now I have to start all over again!" Bruno Ugg said.

"You see how it is," Loretta Fischetti said. "What's your name?"

"Call me Nick," I said.

"Nick? That's your name?"

"Not my real name."

"No?"

"No. It's my nickname."

"I see. Your nickname is Nick."

"That's right."

"What's your real name?"

"Do you have to know?"

"Yes. We have to know."

"My real name is Ivan."

"Ivan what?"

"Ivan Itch."

"Your name is Itch? Ivan Itch? Are you telling the truth?"

"Yes. It was a longer name that ended in *itch*, and my great-grandfather shortened it."

"Because he thought it sounded funny?"

"Yes."

"So he shortened it to *Itch*?"

"I think he was dyslexic."

"And then your parents named you Ivan?"

"Ivan was my great-grandfather's name."

"What do you think of this guy?" Loretta Fischetti asked Bruno Ugg.

"He can hang out with us. Oh, dang! I talked!" Bruno Ugg looked at his watch and made a note on a little piece of paper. He was recording the time he had begun his vow of silence—again.

6

S o what are you guys doing down here?" I asked.
"Are you kidding? It's another scorcher out there. People are frying eggs," Loretta Fischetti said. "We're keeping cool underground. So you read *The Count of Monte Cristo?*"

"Just the Classics Comic," I said.

"That's what I meant," Loretta Fischetti said.

"Alexandre Dumas wrote the story—I forget who drew the pictures," I said. "I—that is, my father—has *The Three Musketeers* and *The Man in the Iron Mask*, also by him."

"Could we read them?" Bruno Ugg asked. "Oh, stinkfish! I talked again!" He made another note on his little piece of paper.

"I'll go get them," I said.

"Bring all you've got," Loretta Fischetti said. "We can swap around."

"Not for keeps," I said. "They're really my dad's."

The whole time we were talking, there was this amazing music playing on an old radio Loretta and Bruno had in the basement. It was music I knew I had never heard before, and yet it all sounded familiar, one song after another. It was a little difficult paying attention to what we were saying because of the music, and in fact we had been speaking slower than we might have normally.

"What is this music?" I asked Loretta Fischetti.

"That's Radio Jolly Roger," she said. "It's a pirate radio station. The guy who runs it plays only songs from the past . . . old blues, cowboy songs, hillbilly music, stuff like that. It's cool, isn't it?"

Just then we heard a voice over the radio: "That was Crab Apple Blues' by Memphis Melvin, and this is WRJR, Radio Jolly Roger, in beautiful Hoboken, where the sewer meets the sea, bringing you the finest in recorded music."

"That's Vic Trola," Loretta Fischetti said. "He's my favorite disc jockey on WRJR."

"He's the only disc jockey on WRJR," Bruno Ugg said.

"No he's not," Loretta Fischetti said. "There's Boppin' Bob, and Doctor Secundra Dass, the classical music guy."

"They're all the same person! They're all him! And I spoke again and ruined my vow of silence, blast it!" Bruno Ugg said.

"That's Bruno's theory," Loretta Fischetti said. "He might be right. Anyway, Vic Trola is my favorite."

"He's got a multiple personality. Oops! Doggone it!" Bruno Ugg said, and once more scratched out the starting time on the little piece of paper and wrote in a new one.

"I'll go get my dad's Classics Comics," I said.

"It would be a nice gesture if you brought bottles of Dr. Pedwee's Grape Soda, available at the corner store, on the way back," Loretta Fischetti said. "I think I have some money somewhere."

"It will be my treat," I said.

"I'd like Dr. Pedwee's Raspberry," Bruno Ugg said. Then he said, "Oh, heck!"

"Why did you want to take a vow of silence, anyway?" I asked Bruno Ugg.

"Just to see if I could do it. . . . Dagnabbit! I spoke again!"

"I'll be back in a few," I said.

7

The radio in the little corner store was playing a cowboy song. I guessed it was that same radio station. Then I heard Vic Trola announce, "That was 'Blood on the Saddle,' sung by Tex Ritter." It was Radio Jolly Roger, all right.

There was a counter with five stools, a display case full of candy bars, a wall rack with newspapers in English, Italian, Spanish, German, and some other languages that use different alphabets, Arabic maybe, or Hebrew, or Russian. I recognized Chinese. There was a fan, like the one in my bedroom, turning left and right, blowing the hot air around. On shelves there was everything from soap powder and dog food to spark plugs and panty hose.

There was a redheaded guy behind the counter. He stuck out his hand.

"Welcome to my little shop, fine young gentleman. I am Sean Vergessen."

I shook his hand. "Call me Nick," I said.

"That your real name?" Sean Vergessen asked.

"Why wouldn't it be?" I asked.

"I don't know," Sean Vergessen said. "I just thought it might be a . . . nickname." He giggled.

"I want a bottle of Dr. Pedwee's Grape Soda, a bottle of Dr. Pedwee's Raspberry, and a bottle of . . ."

"May I suggest Dr. Pedwee's Grapefruit-Lime," Sean Vergessen said. "It's refreshing and delightful. By the way, you've never been in here before, have you?"

"We just moved in," I said.

"Oh! You're the kid who had his bike stolen!" Sean Vergessen said.

"How did you know that?" I asked, surprised.

"I hear things," Sean Vergessen said.

"Do you know who took it?" I asked.

"Tell you what, young Nick," Sean Vergessen said. "Since you are new to the neighborhood and this is your first time in my store, the sodas are on the house, and here's a bag of fried pork rinds, also free." He put the bottles and the bag of pork rinds into my backpack, into which I had already put my father's collection of Classics Comics.

"So do you know who took my bike?" I asked.

"Well, I have to go in the back and . . . count things," Sean Vergessen said. "I'm sure you have many things to do also."

The next thing I knew, I was outside in the street.

8

The basement in Loretta Fischetti's and Bruno Ugg's building wasn't dark and full of stuff like mine. There was linoleum on the floor and hideous blue-green paint on the walls. There were a couple of beat-up sofas and a big easy chair, also crummy. There was a washing machine and a dryer, and of course the old radio. Light came from fluorescent tubes on the ceiling. Bruno and Loretta had their Classics Comics in a plastic milk crate.

"I'm back," I said. "I have sodas."

"Gimme," Bruno Ugg said.

"Give up on the vow of silence?" I asked.

"It wasn't working out," Bruno said. "Loretta kept tricking me into talking."

"I'm twice as smart as he is," Loretta said. "Tricking him is pathetically easy."

"That being the case," Bruno said, "I don't see what pleasure it gives you to mess with my head."

"It's my way of showing affection," Loretta said. "Are the pork rinds for us?"

"Help yourselves," I said. "Sean Vergessen gave me the whole works for free, because I'm new."

"Nice gesture," Bruno Ugg said.

"Say, what's the deal with Sean Vergessen?" I asked.

"What do you mean?" Loretta Fischetti asked back.

"Is he all right, or what?"

"Well, for an adult, I'd say he's pretty all right."

"How come he didn't want to talk about who stole my bike?" I asked.

"Ohhh, you're the one whose bike was stolen!"

"Yes, and Vergessen seemed to know all about it, but he wouldn't say who took it."

"That's because he's D and D," Loretta Fischetti said.

"D and D?" I asked.

"Deaf and Dumb," Loretta Fischetti said. "Old tradition on the waterfront. It's considered bad manners to name names."

"We sort of knew about it too," Bruno Ugg said. "Of course, we didn't know it was your bike exactly."

"Do you know who took it?" I asked. "I'd really like to get it back."

"It's not so much a who as a what," Loretta said.

"A what?"

"Yes. There's a sort of . . . phantom that hangs around."

"A phantom? What do you mean?"

"You know, a mysterious figure, possibly human, possibly something else, lurks in the shadows, menaces people, does things."

"Does things?"

"Like your bike."

"So you think a phantom took it?"

"It's just an educated guess."

"Why not just some normal thief?"

"Well, from what I heard, it's a really crappy bike. What normal thief would want it?"

9

All this time Jolly Roger Radio was playing in the background—guys twanging guitars or blowing on jugs, songs about faithless love, having the blues, herding cattle, and shooting people with a pistol as long as your arm. Bruno Ugg had pulled my father's stack of Classics Comics out of my backpack and was dividing them into two piles—ones they had read already and ones they hadn't.

"It doesn't only do bad things," he said.

"The phantom?"

"Sometimes it leaves little presents," Loretta Fischetti said.

"You'll wake up in the morning, and there on the foot of your bed will be a piece of broken machinery, or a brick, or maybe half a tuna fish sandwich," Bruno Ugg said.

"Has anything like that happened to you personally?" I asked.

"Maybe," Bruno Ugg said.

"D and D," Loretta Fischetti said.

10

"I have dibs on *The Three Musketeers*!" Bruno Ugg said.

"Okay, I'll read *The Man in the Iron Mask*, and then we'll swap," Loretta Fischetti said.

"I'd wait and read *The Three Musketeers* first," I said. *"The Man in the Iron Mask* is sort of a sequel."

"Thanks," Loretta Fischetti said. "Let's see what Jules Verne ones you've got."

"Around the World in Eighty Days."

"Already read it."

"Did you read *Twenty Thousand leagues Under the Sea?*"

"No! Is that by him? I've heard of it."

Loretta Fischetti grabbed my copy of *Twenty Thousand Leagues Under the Sea* and her bottle of Dr. Pedwee's Grape and flopped into the broken-down armchair.

I flipped through the Classics Comics in the milk crate, selected *The Hunchback of Notre Dame* by Victor Hugo, and got comfortable on the sofa that wasn't occupied by Bruno Ugg.

The morning passed like that. While the sidewalks got egg-frying hot, we sprawled in the cool basement, listening to the sweet sounds of Radio Jolly Roger, sipping the sweet sodas, crunching the pork rinds, and turning pages.

After *The Hunchback of Notre Dame*, which was good, I read *Dr. Jekyll and Mr. Hyde*, which was better. Bruno handed over *The Three Musketeers* to Loretta when he was finished, and then read *The Man in the Iron Mask.*

At one point Mrs. Fischetti, Loretta's mother, came down to do laundry. At lunchtime Bruno Ugg's mother brought us bologna sandwiches and glasses of milk.

By midafternoon, about the time I started reading *Oliver Twist*, Loretta Fischetti and Bruno Ugg were my best friends.

11

"What did you do all day, old bean?" my father asked.
"I met a couple of kids on the block."

"Nice blokes?"

"One bloke and one . . . blokette," I said. "And they seem pretty nice. They have even more Classics Comics than you. We've been sort of swapping around, but not for keeps. It's all right, isn't it?"

"Do they have *The Corsican Brothers* by Alexandre Dumas?" my father asked.

"I don't know," I said.

"If they have it, ask if I may borrow it," my father said. "It's a cracking good yarn."

"Dad, are you English?"

"Why no, old thing. I was born in Jersey City, as you very well know. Why do you ask?"

"No reason. Is it okay if I go with my friends tonight? We're going to try to catch bats."

"Bats are tricky little blighters. See that you don't get rabies and die," my father said.

"Actually, I don't think there's much chance of getting near one. Bruno Ugg—one of my new friends—seems to think you can catch a bat by throwing your hat at it."

"It seems unlikely," my father said. "All the same, if you should get bitten, tell me at once so I can arrange for the series of painful shots."

"Thanks, Dad," I said.

"Have fun, Ivan," my father said.

12

Alexandre Dumas was born in 1802. He was the son of a general in Napoleon's army. His grandmother was a black Haitian slave, and he was proud of her. He was fat, wrote 650 books, had all kinds of adventures, fought in revolutions, hunted big game, had a big yacht, traveled all over, was very rich and spent it all, and was the most famous writer in France and the most famous Frenchman in the world. He died in 1870 and is my father's favorite Classics Comics author. All but that last bit I learned from reading in the back of the Classics Comic of *The Three Musketeers*. I think my father has also read some of Alexandre Dumas's books in the full-length version. I know I am going to tackle *The Man in the Iron Mask* some-day.

13

M y mother was sitting on the floor in the middle of the living room with a rag wrapped around her head. She was taking a break from prying up five layers of crummy linoleum to expose the original crummy wooden flooring.

"Going out?" she asked me.

"Going to catch bats with my new friends," I said.

"See? We just arrived, and already you're doing urban things. You're interacting with urban children. Didn't I tell you moving to Hoboken would be good for you?"

Here's what I was thinking: I am supposedly going to hurl my baseball cap at flying rats who might be rabid, and the fact that I have almost no hope of catching one makes it only slightly less an insane thing to do. Also, while Loretta Fischetti and Bruno Ugg are obviously really nice kids, my mother doesn't know that—we could all be setting out to rob a bank. Finally, the fact that I have agreed to go out at night and play bat-hat should be proof to my mother that I have no will of my own and could be influenced to do any kind of foolish or dangerous thing.

Here's what I said to my mother: "Yes, Mom, you sure were right. Urban life is really interesting."

14

I met Loretta Fischetti and Bruno Ugg in the street. Loretta Fischetti had a beret, and Bruno Ugg had a regular felt snap-brim hat, like people used to wear—you see them in movies. I was wearing my Happy Valley Walruses baseball hat.

The walrus was the mascot of Happy Valley High School, where I'd expected all my life to go. There was an old belief that the early inhabitants would put out to sea by way of the seventy-three-mile-long Shwamapo River and hunt walruses. My father said it was highly unlikely that there were many walruses off the coast of New Jersey, and the early inhabitants were probably smuggling goods off ships without paying the import tax. Just the same, all the Happy Valley High School teams were called the Fighting Walruses, and our grade-school teams were called the Junior Walruses.

"I see you've got your hat," Loretta Fischetti said. "Let's be on our way to the park—it will be dark soon."

As we walked through the streets of Hoboken on the way to the park, I noticed numerous other kids going in the same direction. Loretta Fischetti and Bruno Ugg appeared to know some of the kids and waved or said hello to them. They introduced me to a few. All the other kids were wearing hats.

When we got to the park, I saw at least one hundred kids—probably closer to two hundred. Every one of them was wearing a hat. I saw cowboy hats, derbies, Mexican sombreros, hunting caps with earflaps, beanies, straw farmer hats, fancy ladies' hats with flowers, sailor hats, top hats like the ones magicians pull rabbits out of, cop hats, locomotive engineer hats, slouch hats, fedoras, trilbies, homburgs, Tyroleans, boaters, caps, pith helmets, conical wizard hats, knit ski caps, and paper hats.

"It's the Hoboken Bat Hat Festival," Bruno Ugg said.

The kids were checking out the hats, as I was. They were milling all around the park, and more kids, wearing hats, were arriving every minute.

"What goes on?" I asked.

"As I said, it's the Hoboken Bat Hat Festival," Bruno Ugg said. "On a certain night in the summer, kids show up at this park. Real little kids aren't allowed, and older kids, like high schoolers, don't come either—just us middle kids. One day the word goes around town that tonight is the Bat Hat Festival, and we all come here, wearing hats. It's an ancient tradition that goes back to our walrus fisherman ancestors."

"Walruses are mammals," I said.

"You going to argue with ancient tradition?" Bruno Ugg asked me. "The guys who caught them were called walrus fishermen. I don't make the rules."

"So what happens now?" I asked.

"You will notice that there are street lamps along the paths here in the park" Loretta Fischetti said. "When it gets good and dark, insects are attracted to the street lamps and swarm all around them. And you know what that brings."

"Bats?" I asked.

"Bats. Of course we can't see the bats, because they fly in the darkness above the street lamps, feeding on the insects. When you look at a light, the darkness just beyond it is even darker—and the bats are dark themselves, and fast. So what we do—"

"What we do is," Bruno Ugg said, "we toss our hats up into the darkness, trying to get them above and beyond the street lamps. You toss your hat, and into it flies Mr. Bat. Naturally, once he's in the hat, he can't flap his little leather wings, and the whole thing, bat and hat, comes down to the ground. You pounce on your hat, and bang! you've caught yourself a bat!"

"And then what do you do?" I asked. "What do you do once you've caught the bat?"

Bruno Ugg and Loretta Fischetti looked at each other. Some other kids had gathered around us during the explanation. "What do we do when we catch a bat?" Bruno asked.

"I don't rightly know" Loretta Fischetti said. "No one has ever caught one when I've been here. It's not easy"

"I think someone caught a bat three years ago," Bruno Ugg said.

15

The streetlights had come on, and the purple twilight was turning to blackness. Fireflies blinked in the branches of the trees. The kids spread out along the paths in Tesev Noskecnil Park, named after some hero of the past—probably one of those walrus fishermen, I thought.

Loretta Fischetti, Bruno Ugg, and I staked out a length of path near a streetlight and waited. The others took their hats off, so I did too.

It was getting darker by the second. I could hear kids shouting in different parts of the park.

"The bats are here! The bats are here!"

"I think I saw one! I think I saw one!"

"Hush! Quiet! You have to listen for the squeaking!"

"Shlermie! Where's Shlermie?"

Kids were starting to run back and forth and toss their hats.

"Whoo! Good one!"

"See how high mine went?"

"Shlermie, where are you?"

"I think I got one! I think I got one! I got one! I got one! Awww, rats! I didn't get one!"

"Look! Look! There's a bat! Throw your hat!"

"Hey! My hat is stuck in a tree!"

"Shlermie! Are you here?"

"Will you look out? Quit bumping into me!"

"Euwww! I stepped in something!"

"There's more bats over here!"

"You're standing on my hat!"

"I can't see the bats! Where are they?"

"Here, bats! Nice bats! Come here, bats!"

"Idiot! Bats won't come when you call them!"

"A bat just flew over my head! Really! I swear!"

"Ow! I ran into a tree!"

"Shlermeeee!"

At first I was tossing my hat in the air like all the others. Then, as I ran back and forth and listened to all the shouting, I began to shout too, and then I began to laugh. I noticed that Loretta Fischetti and Bruno Ugg were laughing. Everybody was laughing. After a while I was laughing so hard I couldn't do anything else. I got out of breath and bent over with my hands on my knees, laughing. Then I sank to the ground and just lay there laughing so hard my eyes filled with tears. My stomach muscles hurt from laughing so hard. Just about everyone else was on the ground too, rolling back and forth and waving arms and legs and laughing until all we could do was sort of sob and giggle.

Bruno Ugg was lying near me, flat on his back. He was the first to get control of himself. I heard him say, "The good old Bat Hat Festival. Always a success."

I sat up and was feeling around for my hat when I noticed, at the very edge of the park, barely catching the light from one of the street lamps, a tall figure, very tall, dressed in a long black coat—more of a cape—with a hood. As I watched, the tall figure in black mounted a small girl's bike, light blue, with pink hearts and flowers painted on the frame.

"Look! That . . . that . . . phantom's got my bike!" I said, just as it rode away into the darkness.

16

All over Tesev Noskecnil Park, kids were pulling them-selves together, dusting themselves off, and looking for their hats. They walked out of the park and headed for home down various streets, in twos and threes and little bunches.

"Wow! So you actually saw the phantom!" Bruno Ugg said.

"Well, I saw something that looked to me like a phan-tom," I said. "And it had my bike."

"You lucky pup," Loretta Fischetti said. "Hardly anyone has ever seen the phantom. People just have things stolen or wake up to find a broken toaster oven in their room."

"Or they hear strange noises in the night," Bruno Ugg said. "Excuse me for changing the subject, but do you know who used to live in this house?"

We had just left the park and were at the top of River Street. There was an ordinary brick house, the kind that has three or four apartments. There was an iron fence in front and a little garden.

"No idea," I said. "Was it a walrus fisherman?"

"This house, once upon a time, was the residence of Gugliermo Marconi," Bruno Ugg said proudly.

"And who was that? A rock star?" I asked.

"You mean to stand there and tell us you don't know who Gugliermo Marconi was?" Loretta Fischetti asked.

"Not only do I not know who he was, I have no hope of pronouncing his name," I said. "So who was he already?"

"Did you ever hear of a thing called radio?" Bruno Ugg asked.

"Of course I have heard of a thing called radio," I said. "I suppose you are going to tell me that this Marconi guy invented it."

"Bingo!" Loretta Fischetti said.

"What?" I asked. "No kidding?"

"No kidding."

"That's a pretty big invention," I said. "And he lived here?"

"So we are told," Bruno Ugg said.

The apartment on the first floor had a picture window, and we could see right into the living room. It wasn't a normal living room. It was part living room and part something else. A guy in a white shirt, wearing earphones on his head, was sitting at a sort of table with lights and switches and a big microphone in front of him.

"That wouldn't be the guy himself, would it?" I asked. "He looks kind of goofy to be a famous inventor."

The guy in the earphones was motioning for us to come inside.

"He's no Marconi," Loretta Fischetti said. "This guy is Vic Trola."

We crowded into the apartment. When Vic Trola talked, I recognized his voice immediately.

"Kids, I'm dying for a Dr. Pedwee's Double Fudge. If you'll run over to Washington Street and get me a couple, there's a buck plus three sodas in it for you."

Five minutes later we were back in Vic Trola's combination living room and disk jockey studio with cold bottles of Dr. Pedwee's soda, sitting on the old sofa and watching him do his radio show.

There were cardboard egg cartons stapled all over the walls and ceiling, and it felt like four or five thicknesses of carpet under our feet. That was to absorb noise, Vic Trola explained to us.

Vic Trola held a finger to his lips, signaling us to be quiet. "That was 'Chicken on a Raft Blues' by Blind Fig," he said into the microphone while slipping an old-fashioned non-stereo phonograph record into its brown paper sleeve, sliding out another one, putting it on a turntable, and lowering the tone arm onto the rim.

"Now we'll hear Cowboy Steve and his Chuck Wagon Warblers doing a tune called 'The Old Drooling Drover,'" Vic Trola said while turning the volume up on the turntable, turning the volume down on his microphone, taking a swig of his Dr. Pedwee's, noting the time on his big wall clock, and writing down what record he had just played in his big logbook.

"I have to record everything in the log. Federal regulations," Vic Trola said.

17

Vic Trola pointed to us. "You may talk now," he said. "But when I do this"—he made a throat-cutting motion with his hand—"that means, stop talking at once, okay?"

We nodded silently.

"No, it's okay to talk now," Vic Trola said. "I was just demonstrating. But when I do that again, it's dummy-up time, got it?"

"Mr. Trola," Loretta Fischetti began.

"Call me Vic."

"Vic, we thank you for the sodas and the dollar tip," Loretta Fischetti said. "But why couldn't you go over to Washington Street yourself? It's only a short block."

"Regulations," Vic Trola said. "Federal regulations. I can't leave the radio station unattended when it's broadcasting—in case of a natural disaster, or a shipwreck, or something like that."

"But isn't this a pirate radio station?" Loretta Fischetti asked.

"It sure is," Vic Trola said. "See my flag?"

Tacked to the wall was a black pirate flag with skull and crossed bones and the letters *WRJR*.

"I thought a pirate radio station was unlicensed and illegal," Loretta Fischetti said.

"That is so," Vic Trola said.

"In that case, why do you bother about regulations?"

Vic Trola stood up—actually he crouched, since the cord attaching his headset to the desk wasn't long enough to allow him to stand. "Miss, I may be a pirate, but I am also a gentleman."

"Did Marconi, the inventor of radio, actually live in this house?" I asked.

"Some say that wireless radio was invented by J. C. Bose and Marconi falsely patented it and accepted the Nobel Prize for the other guy's invention. Others say that radio was invented by pixies, but I say . . ." The record on the turntable was coming to the end. Vic Trola made the throat-cutting gesture, turned down the volume on the turntable, turned up the volume on the microphone, and said, "These are the sounds of Radio Jolly Roger, in beautiful Hoboken, where the fish are jumping and the cotton is high. We heard 'Blockhead Breakdown' by the Hogboro Jug Band, followed by 'Little Joe the Wrangler,' sung by William Shatner, after which we heard 'Frozen Yogurt Blues' by Blind Persimmon, and lastly 'Goin' Down Disabled Creek' by the Banjo Buccaneers. Stay tuned to Hoboken's own Radio Jolly Roger, WRJR. We play the songs you long for."

Vic Trola pointed to us again.

"You may talk now," he said.

"You were telling us about Marconi, who may have invented radio and whose house this may once have been," I said.

"Did you know the first organized baseball game was played in Hoboken, in eighteen forty-six?" Vic Trola asked. "And the first steam-driven railroad locomotive in America was built here in eighteen twenty-five. Stephen Foster, the most famous songwriter of the nineteenth century lived here—so did a lot of writers and artists. It has the oldest engineering college, the famous Clam Broth House restaurant, and Frank Sinatra, a big singer, was born here."

18

You know a lot about Hoboken," Bruno Ugg said.

"It's my hobby," Vic Trola said.

"Do you know anything about the phantom?" I asked.

"What?"

"The phantom. Do you know anything about it?"

"Sorry, kids. You have to go," Vic Trola said.

"We have to go? We haven't finished our Dr. Pedwee's!"

"Take them with you. Sorry. You can't hang around the radio station. Federal regulations." Vic Trola was waving his arms at us, shooing us out the door.

The next thing we knew we were outside in the street.

"Bye-bye, kids!" Vic Trola shouted as he pulled the curtains across the picture window. "Keep listening to Radio Jolly Roger!"

"That was a little weird," I said.

"Yes, he was perfectly talkative and friendly until we mentioned the phantom," Loretta Fischetti said.

"Then he couldn't get rid of us fast enough," Bruno Ugg said.

"He went D and D," Loretta Fischetti said.

"Yes, Deaf and Dumb," I said.

19

C - that's the way you begin.
H - is the next letter in.
I - I am the third.
C - Is the middle of the word.
K - I'm fillin'in.
E - I'm near the end.
C-h-i-c-k-e-n,
That's the way you spell chicken.

That was the song we heard on Radio Jolly Roger. It was hot again, so we had gone underground to listen to music and read Classics Comics in the basement of the building where Loretta Fischetti and Bruno Ugg lived.

"*C-h-i-c-k-e-n*, that's the way you spell chicken." They had to be the dumbest words to any song, ever. But the tune was so good, and the guy who sang the song was so good, that it kept going through my mind. Apparently Vic Trola liked it too, because he played it every fifteen or twenty minutes.

"That song is starting to drive me crazy," Loretta Fischetti said.

"I—I am de thoid," Bruno Ugg sang, imitating the guy on the record. "C—in de middle of de woid."

I was reading *Murders in the Rue Morgue* by Edgar Allan Poe. This is an outstanding Classics Comic in which a

French detective named C. Auguste Dupin matches wits with a monster murderer who does horrible crimes in Paris, France. Dupin figures out that the killer is not a human being at all, but an evil ape. He tracks it down in the end. I suspect the comic version does not do the story justice, although it does show lots of blood and scary things.

Bruno Ugg was reading *Moby Dick* by Herman Melville, which I had read previously—it's the story of a loony sea captain and a white whale. It is one of the top stories on my Nick's Picks list, and I recommend it highly. One of the characters is a cannibal.

Loretta Fischetti was reading *Don Quixote* by Miguel de Cervantes, a classic of Spanish literature, and also about a loony old man.

And of course Vic Trola was with us by radio, playing the chicken song in between the old rock 'n' roll, hillbilly songs, and blues.

When I told my mother that I was lunching courtesy of either Bruno Ugg's mother or Loretta Fischetti's mother, she said that she ought to at least provide dessert and gave me some money for the purpose. Only we decided to have dessert first—in today's case it was Dreamsicles. Dreamsicles, for those unfortunate enough not to know, are like Popsicles, only the outside is orange sherbet and the middle is vanilla ice cream. They are very nice on a hot morning, while enjoying music and literature.

"This is all very nice," Loretta Fischetti said. "But I am getting a little fed up with just lying down here like reptiles. We ought to do something."

20

Do what? It's not even ten A.M., and people are being roasted alive," Bruno Ugg said.

"Just the same, I feel like getting out of here," Loretta Fischetti said.

"Are you nuts? You'll be a french fry," Bruno Ugg said.

"I don't know,' Loretta Fischetti said. "Nick could invite us over to see his basement."

"I have an idea," I said. "Why don't we all go over to my basement?"

"Yes? What's over there that's so good?" Loretta Fischetti asked me.

"Just a lot of old junk," I said. "But you were the one who suggested we go over there."

"No, I suggested you invite us," Loretta Fischetti said. "What sort of old junk?"

"All kinds. Lots of it," I said.

"Books, comics, periodicals?" Bruno Ugg asked.

"I don't know," I said. "Probably. There's everything else there. That's where I found the giant fan."

"The one that gives you the radical hairdo," Loretta Fischetti said.

Loretta had decided that the windblown look was cool.

"That's right. There's a lot of busted and rusted machinery, old furniture, tools, boxes of assorted stuff."

"Let's go there," Bruno Ugg said.

"Yes, let's," I said.

"Nothing is stopping us," Loretta Fischetti said.

21

I had scrounged around my basement a bit, but I had hardly made a dent. There were dark corners and stuff underneath stuff. With my friends, Loretta Fischetti and Bruno Ugg, who had brought along a couple of flashlights, a whole world of junk and treasure turned up.

Here are a few of the things we found:

The stuffed swordfish I mentioned before.

Also a stuffed barracuda.

A lot of busted furniture.

An old-time radio in a wooden cabinet—a floor model, about half the size of a refrigerator. We plugged it in, and after warming up for a while, it played! We tuned in Radio Jolly Roger—Vic Trola was playing the how-to-spell-*chicken* song, of course. The radio sounded great and had a neat red light in the dial.

A canoe! A real canoe! It had a big hole in it, but Bruno Ugg thought we might be able to fix it with a piece of tin from a flattened-out big tomato can and some duct tape.

Four wheels, and all four fenders, plus a door from a small foreign car. There was enough debris piled up that there was a chance we'd find the rest of the car if we kept looking.

Six very old-looking vacuum cleaners.

A bathtub.

An iron potbelly stove.

A cool statue of a tall skinny bird around five feet high and covered with gold—or gold paint.

Fencing foils and masks. We put these aside to clean up and play with later. *The Three Musketeers* was pretty much our group favorite Classics Comic, and these were the best things we had found so far.

Then there were boxes. We found a box completely full of used lightbulbs. Some of them rattled when we shook them and some didn't. We found a box full of white coffee mugs—must have been at least sixty of them. We found a box of old clothes, a box of empty bottles, and a box of cracked and mismatched dishes and bowls.

And then, pay dirt! The mother lode! A box of old comics and magazines. It was too dark to really study what was in it. We dragged it under one of the lights and could see titles like Action Comics, Detective Comics, also old *Life* magazines and paperback books.

"Let's take this back to our basement, which isn't so creepy and dirty, and examine everything," Loretta Fischetti said.

Bruno Ugg and I found some rope, tied it around the box so we'd have something to grab, and together we dragged and lifted it up the stairs, out into the street, and then into Bruno's and Loretta's basement.

22

The *Life* magazines were from the 1950s and 1960s. We didn't know how old the comics were—pretty old, we guessed, maybe from the 1940s, some of them. There was a calendar from 1984 and a newspaper from 1991.

Some of the paperback books—mostly science fiction—had dates in the 1950s printed on that page in the front with all the information. It was mostly pretty old stuff.

"I bet these are worth something," Bruno Ugg said.

"What, old comic books and paperbacks? I doubt it," I said. "But they're interesting."

The comics weren't Classics Comics, but they looked promising. Some of them had Superman and Batman stories. We decided we would add them to our little collection.

Then we found the scrapbook.

23

It was bound in brown suede leather, sort of fat and floppy, and held together with thick brown cord. Printed on the leather in black marker were the words CHICKEN EMERGENCY.

The pages had a covering of some kind of thin clear plastic, and newspaper clippings were neatly trimmed and pasted to the pages.

The first clipping was a picture of a white-haired guy with a big scissors, cutting a ribbon over a manhole. The caption read MAYOR DEDICATES NEW SEWER.

Next was an article without a picture: CLAM FEVER SCARE OVER! "WAS MERELY OVEREATING," SAYS DOCTOR.

Then there was a picture of a first-grade class at Hoboken Elementary that had made a giant map of New Jersey out of empty cigarette packages.

"Nothing about a chicken emergency," Bruno Ugg said.

"Look at this article!" I said.

TERROR ON GARDEN STREET

Huge White Creature Sighted by Many

Residents of Garden Street report seeing a very large white animal last night. The animal, which some witnesses identified as a polar bear, was seen running down the street. Other Hoboken residents claim the animal was a white gorilla, because of its ability to climb trees.

Hoboken dog warden Augie Manicotti, asked for comment, said, "All I know is it's not a dog, so it's not my problem."

In addition to a dog warden, Hoboken has a pussycat warden (an unpaid position) and a rat control officer. These individuals also claimed that their duties did not extend to dealing with animals estimated to be over six feet and well over 200 pounds.

Local zoos and circuses were contacted. None
reported losing either a polar bear or a white
gorilla.

"Interesting," Loretta Fischetti said.
"Turn the page," Bruno Ugg said.

HUGE WHITE ANIMAL TERROR CONTINUES
More Sightings Throughout the City

Many citizens report having seen the very large white creature, first thought to be a polar bear or a white gorilla, but there are many opinions concerning just what kind of animal it is.

"It is a tall, fat man in a white fur coat," Mrs. Gloria Gluckstern, proprietress of Lucky Stars Hairdressers and Pizzeria of River Street, said. "My uncle had a coat like that—and he used to run through the streets too."

Kevin Mookerjee of Washington Street said, "It is a yeti, also known as the Abominable Snowman. We have them in the Himalayas. I often saw them when I was a boy in India."

"It's a big friendly dog," said editor Ed Weiss of Fourteenth Street. "I gave it a doughnut."

Hoboken health commissioner Dr. Milton Sargon of Washington Street believes the white apparition does not exist at all. "Mass hysteria," Dr. Sargon said. "Possibly brought on by the consumption of bad clam juice. People expect to see it, so they see it."

When questioned, Dr. Sargon admitted he had seen it himself.

Hoboken mayor Lawrence Vasolini spoke to the press in his office: "The animal, or fat man in a white fur coat, or group hallucination has done no one any harm. I urge the citizens of Hoboken to remain calm. Do not panic!"

CITIZENS PANIC!

Sightings Continue—Populace Freaks Out

Groups of Hoboken residents are wandering the streets, armed with sticks, baseball bats, fishnets, and three-foot-long hard salamis, looking for the white animal that has menaced the town for several nights.

Steve Nickelson, popular man-about-town and patron of the arts, leads one of these vigilante gangs. "We plan to capture the creature," Nickelson said. "We don't care how long it takes or how much salami we have to eat. We will take back our streets from this white monster."

Captain Hook's Book Nook on Newark Street reports that all copies of *Moby Dick* by Herman Melville, a story of a white whale, have been sold out. Also sold was the one copy of *I, Moby* by Winkus Winwater, the same story told from the point of view of the whale.

BOY CLAIMS MONSTER IS PET

It's a Giant Chicken, says Arthur Bobowicz

A young resident of Hoboken claims the white monster that has been menacing the city is just a pet chicken that got lost—a very large pet chicken.

"I got her from Professor Mazzocchi," Arthur Bobowicz of 127 Hudson Street told *The Hoboken Evening News*. "He's a mad scientist who lives on Court Street."

The Hoboken City Directory does not list anyone named Mazzocchi, and the Hoboken Yellow Pages has no entries under "Mad Scientist."

"Her name is Henrietta. She ran away, and she's probably scared," young Bobowicz said. "If you see her, be nice to her—and call me. I'll come and get her."

Other persons contacting *The Hoboken Evening News* have claimed the white apparition is the ghost of Alexander Hamilton, a Hudson River walrus, a weather balloon, and the vice president of the United States.

IT IS A CHICKEN!
I Told You So, Says Bobowicz

Hoboken Evening News photographer Mel Snelson has gotten the first photographs of the white monster, and it is a chicken.

"It was eating some potato peelings in the alley behind the Three Star Chinese-American Lunchroom," Snelson said. "I walked right up to it and got four front views, a profile, and one of the chicken walking away. It clucked at me."

(Additional photos on Page 2.)

The mayor's office refused to confirm or deny rumors that a professional chicken catcher, from out of town, hired by the city at considerable expense, had failed to catch the bird.

Asked for comment, young Arthur Bobowicz said, "It's a chicken. It's my chicken. It's not a monster. Her name is Henrietta. She likes potatoes. Be nice to her."

BE NICE TO THE CHICKEN
Experts Claim Kindness Is Needed

Professor Leon Watstein of Stevens Institute of Technology told *The Hoboken Evening News* that the giant chicken is probably insecure and will stop rampaging at night if treated with kindness.

Hoboken health commissioner Dr. Milton Sargon, who is also chief veterinarian for the Port of Hoboken, said, "Watstein is probably right. He studies that sort of thing."

Dr. Hsu Ting Feng, a famous Chinese poultry expert passing through town, stopped by the offices of *The Hoboken Evening News*. "Chickens are very sensitive birds. Possibly something frightened or upset this chicken, causing it to go wild. Friendly overtures and kind treatment will restore harmony."

BE KIND TO CHICKEN CAMPAIGN UNDERWAY
Bird Appears Mollified

Molly Fried of the Woof 'n' Stuff pet shop
told *The Hoboken Evening News*, "Several people
have purchased the special Chicken Mollifying
Kits we have prepared, which contain potatoes,
potato chips, a chicken hand puppet, and a
sheet of instructions indicating a few basic
and easy-to-learn clucking sounds. Those who
have met the chicken say she seems to be somewhat mollified, or soothed in temper or dis-
position."

147

KID CATCHES BIRD
Henrietta Returns to Bobowicz

Arthur Bobowicz had just gone to bed when Henrietta appeared on the fire escape outside his window. He opened the window and let her in, hugged her, and scratched her head. Henrietta went to sleep on the rug next to Arthur's bed.

In the morning Arthur's mother, Mrs. Beatrice Bobowicz, made home-fried potatoes for Henrietta. Arthur's younger brother and sister, Henry and Lucille, played with the giant chicken. Arthur's father, Mr. Gepetto Bobowicz, telephoned Mayor Vasolini to say that Henrietta had come home.

"The crisis is over," Mayor Vasolini is quoted as saying. "All city departments conducted themselves with professionalism, and we all learned something about being nice to chickens. I told the kid to bring the bird down to city hall to get a chicken license and have his picture taken with me, your mayor."

"S ome story!" Bruno Ugg said.
"I want to meet this Arthur Bobowicz kid," I said. "I want to meet the chicken."

"How do you know he's a kid?" Loretta Fischetti asked. "He might be all grown up by now."

"I know he's a kid because there's his picture from the newspaper. He looks like he's about our age, maybe a year or two younger," I said.

"That newspaper could be years old," Loretta Fischetti said. "Arthur could be an adult, and the chicken could be dead. How long do chickens live, anyhow?"

Loretta had a point. Whoever had made the scrapbook had neatly cut out the articles and pictures and had trimmed off the part of each page that shows the date, and there were no dates added in pen or pencil.

"I think he's still a kid," Bruno Ugg said. "The pictures don't look like they were taken a long time ago. I mean, the people are wearing normal clothes. It looks like now."

"Easy enough to find out," Loretta Fischetti said. "People will remember something as unusual as a giant chicken rampaging through the streets. We can just ask our parents when it happened."

"While you're at it, ask them if they know where Henrietta is and if we can see her," I said.

"Yes. Let's do that," Bruno Ugg said.

33

There ain't nobody here but us chickens
There ain't nobody here at all
So calm yourself and stop that fuss
There ain't nobody here but us
We chickens tryin' to sleep
And you butt in
And hobble hobble hobble hobble with
*   your shin*

Loretta Fischetti asked her mother if she remembered a time when a giant chicken was loose in Hoboken.

"I don't know what you're talking about," Mrs. Fischetti said.

Loretta asked her father.

"I refuse to answer," her father said. "I didn't see anything, and I didn't hear anything."

There ain't nobody here but us chickens
There ain't nobody here at all
You're stomping around, shaking the ground
You're kicking up an awful dust
We chickens tryin' to sleep
And you butt in
And hobble hobble hobble hobble—it's a sin

Bruno Ugg asked his mother if she remembered anything about a giant chicken.

"I mind my own business," Mrs. Ugg said. "I know nothing. Nothing."

Bruno asked his father.

"What's a chicken?" Mr. Ugg said.

I, Nick, also known as Ivan, saw no point in asking my parents, since we'd all just moved to Hoboken. Instead, I asked Sean Vergessen, proprietor of the little corner store what he knew about Henrietta the giant chicken.

"I am D and D, kid," Sean Vergessen said. "And anything I might have known, I've already forgotten. Have a free Dr. Pedwee's Avocado-Lime Soda."

Tomorrow is a busy day
We got things to do
We got eggs to lay
We got ground to dig
And worms to scratch
It takes a lot of settin' gettin' chicks to hatch

"Well, the adults aren't talking," I said.

"We should have warned you," Bruno Ugg said. "It's a Hoboken tradition. Nobody ever gives information in response to a direct question."

"Why is that?" I asked.

"Don't ask me," Bruno Ugg said.

"I have no idea what you're talking about," Loretta Fischetti said.

34

I was born in Hoboken
H-O-B-O-K-E-N
Where the guys are the squarest
The girls are the fairest
H-O-B-O-K-E-N

"Seriously, why won't the adults talk about the chicken?" I asked Loretta Fischetti and Bruno Ugg.

"Not sure," Bruno said. "Maybe it's because they're embarrassed."

"Embarrassed?"

"Yes," Loretta Fischetti said. "I mean, you live in a town where the local disaster wasn't a flood or an earthquake or a hurricane, but a rampage by a giant chicken. It's the sort of thing you want other people to forget about."

"I don't know—it seems sort of cool to me," I said. "I still want to find Arthur Bobowicz and find out what happened to the chicken. In fact, I want to even more now."

"So because the adults don't want to tell us, you want to find out even more?" Bruno Ugg said.

"That's right. You know, that might be a neat way for teachers to motivate kids . . . refuse to teach them."

"Oh, that's right—you haven't been to school in Hoboken yet," Loretta Fischetti said.

"They thought of it already?" I asked.

"Did they ever," Loretta Fischetti said.

"Well, I thought of something," I said. "I thought of a way to get all the info on the chicken. All we have to do is go to *The Hoboken Evening News* and look at the files. Newspapers keep records."

"Newspapers that are still in business do," Bruno Ugg said.

"It's closed down?"

"Closed and gone. It's a Barstuck's Coffee Bistro now."

"Hmmm."

35

"We can ask the police. Police keep records," I said. "I have been wanting to go to the police station anyway, to report the theft of my bicycle."

"I've never been inside the police station," Bruno Ugg said.

"Neither have I," said Loretta Fischetti. "And it's just around the corner."

"Let's go," I said.

The police station was sort of underneath the city hall. We went down a couple of steps into a big room that was dark and cool. It looked just like in the movies. There was a big high desk, and there was a policeman sitting behind it. We stood in front of it, and he had to lean forward and look down to see us.

"I'm Sergeant Flooney," the policeman said. "How can the Hoboken Police Department serve and/or protect youse kids?"

"There are two things," I said. "First of all, I want to report that my bike was stolen."

Sergeant Flooney twisted around in his chair and hollered over his shoulder, "Hey, Spooney! Here's kids to report another stolen bike!" Then he turned back to us, and said, "Go over there, in a minute, and tell Officer Spooney what the bike looked like. Now what was the other thing?"

"Can you tell us anything about the giant chicken?" I asked.

"Chickens aren't a police matter," Sergeant Flooney said. "You want to see the dog warden, or maybe the pussycat warden. Now go and tell Officer Spooney all about your bicycle."

"This was a giant chicken," I said. "It rampaged through the streets."

Sergeant Flooney ran his finger down the page of a big book on his desk. "I don't see any rampages on the blotter," he said. "Like I said, chickens would be some other department. Now go see Officer Spooney. He's waiting to help you."

I told Officer Spooney about my bicycle.

"Light blue with pink hearts?" Officer Spooney asked, writing it all down. "Well try to find it for you, but don't get your hopes up."

"Have there been a lot a bicycles stolen?" Loretta Fischetti asked Officer Spooney.

"A fair number," Officer Spooney said. "We think it's the phantom."

"The phantom?" we all asked at once.

"Did I say *phantom*? I meant to say *family*. We think it may be a family of bicycle thieves. You know, momma, poppa, kiddies—all hardened criminals. They steal 'em, paint them different colors, and sneak them onto ships—sell them in South America."

"Mine was one of those minibikes—a girl's model," I said.

"And you want it back, huh?" Officer Spooney said.

"It's the principle of the thing," I said.

"Write down your phone number," Officer Spooney said. "We'll call you if we have any news."

36

"Officer Spooney said *phantom*," Bruno Ugg said when we were outside the police station. "Then he tried to cover it up."

"So it was the phantom who stole my bike! I suspected as much!" I said.

"And he or she has stolen other bikes too," Loretta Fischetti said.

"And the adults don't want to talk about it," I said.

"Just like the giant chicken," Bruno Ugg said.

"What is it with the adults around here?" I asked.

"I'm saying nothing," Loretta Fischetti said.

"I refuse to answer," Bruno Ugg said.

"Well, I bet I know one person who could tell us all about everything," I said.

"Who's that?"

"Arthur Bobowicz."

"Well, he should at least be able to tell us about the chicken," Loretta Fischetti said. "But you know what?"

"What?" Bruno Ugg and I asked.

"This morning I looked up Arthur Bobowicz in the phone directory."

"And?"

"There was no Arthur Bobowicz," Loretta Fischetti said. "There was no Bobowicz, even. So you have any ideas?"

"I do have an idea, now that you mention it," I said. "Your parents and Sean Vergessen told us nothing," I said. "The newspaper is shut down. Sergeant Flooney and Officer Spooney we just met, and they were no help. But I have an idea. There is one place where you can always get information, and that place is . . ."

"Yes? That place is? Tell us!" Loretta Fischetti said.

"That place is . . .," I said. I paused again, just to tease the others.

"Spit it out, Nick!" Bruno Ugg shouted. "What is that place where you can always get information?"

Smiling broadly because it was such a neat idea and I had thought of it, I said, "That place is . . . the public library!"

"Novel notion," Bruno Ugg said.

"I confess, it would not have occurred to me," Loretta Fischetti said.

"Let's go there right now," I said. "Where is it, by the way?"

"I'm pretty sure I know where it is," Loretta Fischetti said. "Let's go."

37

"Yes, the good old public library," I said as Loretta Fischetti led us along the broiling hot streets of Hoboken. "Repository of knowledge and learning. Treasure house of stories and poetry. The intellectual record and cultural memory of the community. Temple of wisdom." I got all this stuff off the back of my old library card from Happy Valley.

"Here we are," Loretta Fischetti said.

The Hoboken Public Library looked a little like Dracula's house in the Classics Comic. It was old-fashioned and beaten up. There were green wooden shutters over some of the windows. Some of the shutters were missing, some were broken, and some were hanging crookedly The steps leading up to the big, black wooden door were covered with pigeon poop. I was about to suggest that maybe the library had closed and moved away when I saw the little black wooden sign with gold letters painted on it: LIBRARY IS OPEN.

We pushed open the big black door and went inside. There was a funny musty odor, like stale cornflakes. Everything inside the library was made of marble or wood painted to look like marble. The ceiling was high, and a dim gray light came from a round skylight in the middle of it. The glass of the skylight was dirty, and there appeared to be the shadow of a dead pigeon. There didn't seem to be any people in the building.

Then we heard a voice. We knew in less than a second that it was the voice of a crazy person.

"Who enters my library?" the crazy voice called. "Stand perfectly still! I warn you that I am expert in akido, bar-itsu, boxing, fencing, Greco-Roman wrestling, jiujitsu, judo, karate, kendo, savate, tai chi, and yubi-waza—so you are helpless against me. Now let me see what kind of vandals and hooligans are here."

Through an open doorway, we saw someone coming upstairs from the basement of the library. It was a woman with wild hair, wearing what looked like a gym suit with rainbow-striped leg warmers and a cape.

"Ah! It is children!" the woman said. "And fairly harm-less looking. What do you wish, children? Do you know where you are? This is a li-bra-ry. Do you know what that is?"

"We know what a library is," I said. "We wish to get some information."

The crazy lady in the rainbow leg warmers staggered and steadied herself against a desk. "Well! That took me by surprise! Information, you say. Well, information you shall have. I am Starr Lackawanna, the official librarian, custodian, and night watchperson. How may I help you?"

"We wanted to find out about the giant chicken," I said.

"Certainly, children. Nothing easier. And there is just time to do the research. I am closing the library early today. President Harry S. Truman is going to speak down at the ferry terminal, and I am going to hear him. Now just wait there. I will be back with your giant chicken informa-tion in two shakes of a lamb's tail."

Starr Lackawanna hurried off into the dark recesses of the library.

"Am I mistaken, or is she crazy as a bat?" I asked.

"You're not mistaken," Loretta Fischetti said.

"And wasn't Harry S.Truman the president a long time ago?" Bruno Ugg asked.

"Long time ago," I said.

"But at least she didn't dummy up when we wanted to know about the giant chicken," Loretta Fischetti said.

"That's true," I said. "Finally we're making some progress."

Starr Lackawanna was back. "I found what you wanted to know," she said. "Would you care to borrow pencils to take notes? I have some scratch paper you may use."

Starr Lackawanna led us to a big table and gave us pencils and scraps of paper. "The common name of the chicken is the Jersey Giant," she began. "It is also known as the Jersey Black Giant, but its scientific name is *Gallus domesticus,* like all chickens. It is an American chicken . . . and it is much larger than others."

This was great. Loretta Fischetti, Bruno Ugg, and I were scribbling madly as Starr Lackawanna spoke.

"The Black brothers developed the Jersey Giant here in New Jersey in the eighteen seventies. The 'black' in its name is the surname of its creators, the Black brothers. The bird comes in three varieties, black, blue, and white."

We nodded to each other. The pictures in the scrapbook had been of a white chicken.

"The Jersey Giant reaches large sizes, as its name implies. Cocks are generally thirteen pounds, hens are ten pounds, cockerels are eleven pounds, and pullets are eight pounds. They are the largest breed in the American class."

We were confused.

"Thirteen pounds? That's as big as they get?" we asked Starr Lackawanna.

"As I understand things, that is as big as any chicken in America gets," the eccentric librarian said.

"So this Jersey Giant would not stand well over six feet, would it?" we asked.

"Oh, no, children. I imagine they would be oh . . . so high." Starr Lackawanna indicated with her hand. "I hope this has been of some help, children. Now I must ask you to leave the library. We don't want to be late and miss the president's speech, do we?"

Starr Lackawanna hustled us out of the library.

"Come back again any time," she said. "Any time you want information—that's what I'm here for." She locked the big door and hurried down the street with her cape flowing out behind her and her rainbow leg warmers flashing.

"Different giant chicken," Bruno Ugg said.

"Yep, different chicken," I said.

38

Everybody's talking about chicken
Chicken's a popular bird
Anywhere you go, you're bound to find
A chicken ain't nothin' but a bird

"Dad, this is a long shot, but do you know anything about a giant chicken?"

"Do you suppose you could call me Pater? It sounds so nice. And you could call your mother Mater. It's Latin, you know."

"Never mind. I'm sorry I asked."

"Sorry? Sorry you asked about the giant chicken that terrorized Hoboken some time ago?"

"What? You know about it?" I was wild with excitement.

"Well, of course I know about it, old fig," my father said. "It was in the newspaper."

"Tell me all you remember . . . Pater," I said.

"Let me see. . . . There was this huge white creature storming about in the streets. People didn't know what to make of it—thought it was a polar bear and all sorts of things. Then it turned out to be an outlandish huge chicken. There was some more carrying on, and in the end it turned out to have been some child's pet. Ridiculous, eh? Much ado about nothing. Mind you, it was an exceptionally large chicken."

"Do you remember when all this happened?" I asked my father.

"No idea, old waffle," my father said. "Whoever had put together the scrapbook had trimmed off the part of the page that shows the date."

"The scrapbook?" I asked.

"Yes. I was rummaging in the basement a few weeks ago and found a box of old rubbish. There was a scrapbook with cuttings about the chicken. I can find it for you, if you like."

"So all you know about the chicken is what you read in that scrapbook."

"I just said," my father said. "What's the matter, old egg, you look rather disappointed."

"My friends and I found that same scrapbook," I said. "We've been trying to find out more about the chicken and the kid, Arthur Bobowicz. Also, there seems to be some sort of phantom. I think it stole my bicycle. The thing is, when we ask adults about this stuff, they don't know anything or they won't tell us what they do know. For a minute I thought you knew about the chicken and were going to tell me something."

"I see your problem," my father said. "It's deuced frustrating. You know, most adults don't feel they have time to answer the questions of you little whippersnappers. But I can tell you how to get all the local news and gossip."

"How?" I asked.

"It's simply a matter of who you ask. As I said, most adults won't give you the time of day—but here's what you must do. Look for a shabby individual, one who is a bit dirty, needs a shave, and doesn't smell very nice. This chap will often be sitting on a bench in the park. You may notice that he has a bottle of wine in a paper bag."

"A bum?" I asked.

"So to speak," my father said. "Now here's someone who has plenty of time to observe the passing parade. He's generally ignored by the rest of society—nobody wants to hear anything he may have to say. You give this fellow your respectful attention, and possibly fifty cents, and he will tell you everything he knows."

"So ask a bum in the park?"

"Do remember that some people who fit the description are psychotic and might possibly attack you. But if you're polite, keep a safe distance, and your eye on a route of escape, you should be all right. About the worst thing that may happen will be having a small wine bottle bounced off your noggin. On the positive side, you might have an interesting conversation."

"So you're recommending this?" I asked my father.

"Oh, absolutely old nut. I talk to homeless chappies all the time myself," my father said. "Fine fellows, mostly."

On my way out the door, my mother called to me. She was on a tall ladder, chipping paint off the ceiling.

"Everything all right?" my mother asked. "Doing anything interesting?"

"I'm going to meet my friends. We're going to start conversations with alcoholic homeless men in the park," I said.

"It's another urban experience!" my mother said. "My boy is meeting life and looking it in the eye! Have a good time, Ivan!"

In the Big Rock Candy Mountain
The cops have wooden legs
The bulldogs all have rubber teeth
And the hens lay soft-boiled eggs

It didn't take us long to find Meehan the Bum. He was sitting on a bench just inside Tesev Noskecnil Park.

"He's perfect," Loretta Fischetti said. I had told her my father's requirements for a suitable bum—shabby, dirty, unshaven, bad smelling, bottle of wine in a paper bag. "Let's engage him in conversation."

"Good afternoon, sir," Bruno Ugg said. "I am Bruno Ugg, this is my friend Loretta Fischetti, and this lad we simply call Nick."

"If you're members of the Democratic Party trying to scare up votes, you're wasting your time," the bum said.

"It's nothing like that," I said. "We just wanted to wish you a good afternoon and pass the time of day."

"I am Meehan the Bum," the bum said. "I have always voted a straight Republican ticket, and the park is free to all."

"Rather than get into a discussion of politics," Loretta Fischetti said, "we wondered if you possibly recall the giant chicken that caused such a stir here in Hoboken."

Meehan the Bum took a swig from his bottle of wine and wiped his mouth with the back of his hand. He gazed over our heads, across the park, and up the Hudson River. His eyes were red-rimmed and watery.

"Giant chicken, you say? Aye, I have seen the giant chicken. I have seen the giant chicken of Sumatra, a bird too horrible to speak of. I have seen giant chickens in the hills of Kalimantan Borneo strong enough to carry away a young bullock in their beaks. See this scar?"

Meehan the Bum pointed to the knee of his greasy corduroy trousers. We nodded, although we saw no scar, only dirty fabric.

"I got this scar in a fight with a giant chicken in a back alley in Kowloon. Arr, children, I have seen more giant chickens than you have had hot breakfasts. I've seen them on land and sea, seen them in Africa and Asia and here in the States. I was chased by a giant chicken in Arizona once—had me on the run for four days. I had to climb down one side of the Grand Canyon and up the other. When a giant chicken takes a dislike to you, it's a hard bird to get away from."

"Can you tell us anything about the giant chicken that was here in Hoboken?" I asked.

"Once I was in Ulan Bator. I was having a saucer of fermented mare's milk, when this giant chicken walks up to me.

"'I suppose you think you're better than me,' the giant chicken says.

"'I think nothing of the sort,' I say. 'I am just having a quiet saucer of kumis and a poppy-seed bagel.'

"'I saw the way you looked at me when I came in,' the giant chicken says. 'You Republicans have ruined everything.'

"I can see I am going to have to fight this giant chicken. He's an ugly customer, and I wouldn't be surprised if he pulled a knife or a gun on me. So I say, 'Excuse me, but is that your order of mashed potatoes?' Giant chickens can't resist potatoes. While he is distracted, looking for the potatoes, I klonk him with a bottle and run out the door."

"How about the giant chicken right here in town?" I asked Meehan the Bum. "Have you ever run into her?"

"Well, actually, no," Meehan the Bum said. "This is the first I've heard of it."

"Oh, great," Loretta Fischetti said. "He never heard of the giant chicken. I don't suppose there's any point in asking him about the phantom."

"Why don't you ask me and see?" Meehan the Bum asked.

"All right. I'll play," I said. "Do you know anything about the phantom?"

"Not really," Meehan the Bum said. "Except I do know where the cave is where the phantom keeps the things it steals."

40

"The cave?"

"Yep. Sibyl's Cave," Meehan the Bum said. "Old Hoboken Landmark. That's where the phantom keeps all the stolen goods."

"Wait a minute," Loretta Fischetti said. "I never heard of any cave in Hoboken."

"Well, there is one," Meehan the Bum said. "It used to be a popular tourist attraction. There was a natural spring in the cave, and people used to pay a penny per glass to drink the water—which was a whole lot of money for a glass of water, but they thought the water had medicinal properties. This started in eighteen thirty-two, and went on until the eighteen eighties when Hoboken got a board of health."

"Then what happened?" Bruno Ugg asked.

"Board of health closed it down. Turns out the water wasn't fit for human consumption," Meehan the Bum said.

"I've been all over Hoboken, and I have never seen any cave," Loretta Fischetti said.

"Have you ever played in the baseball field at the other end of this park?" Meehan the Bum asked.

"Yes."

"Then you were standing right on top of the cave. You know that road at the bottom of the cliff, under the baseball field, that goes alongside the river?"

"Frank Sinatra Drive?"

"Well, that's where the entrance to the cave used to be," Meehan the Bum said. "For a while there was an illegal fermented sauerkraut factory in the cave. During the nineteen thirties, this was."

"I never saw any entrance to any cave down there," Loretta Fischetti said.

"That's because they sealed it up and disguised it," Meehan the Bum said. "So kids like you wouldn't wander in and get killed."

"If it's sealed up, how does the phantom get in?" Loretta Fischetti asked. "Assuming that I believe a single word you're saying—which I do not."

"There's a secret entrance," Meehan the Bum said. "Unless you knew it was there, you'd never find it. That's how the phantom goes in and out."

"And you know where the entrance is," I said.

"That's right," Meehan the Bum said. "And I won't tell where—but I'll give you a hint: Trust Buster."

"Who's Buster?" Bruno Ugg said.

"I'm dummied up," Meehan the Bum said. "Find out for yourselves."

"We're going to check on this story, you know," Loretta Fischetti said.

"Feel free," Meehan the Bum said. "But if you ask those Democrats, they'll just lie to you. Once, in Arizona, a big Democrat chased me for four days. I had to climb down one side of the Grand Canyon and up the other. Finally we had it out in an alley. I was afraid he would pull a knife or a gun on me. . . ."

"He's off again," Bruno Ugg said.

"Good-bye, Mr. Meehan," I said. "Thank you for talking to us."

"Big giant chickens," Meehan the Bum said. "I've seen them on five continents. Big, mean, crazy giant chickens."

Loretta Fischetti, Bruno Ugg, and I walked quietly away and out of the park.

41

"Well, he's certainly nuts," Bruno Ugg said as we walked down Washington Street.

"The stuff about the cave is interesting," Loretta Fischetti said. "I'd like to know if it really exists."

"How would we find out?" I asked.

"We could go back to the library," Bruno Ugg said.

"Starr Lackawanna?" I asked. "Would she be able to tell us?"

"She said to come back any time we wanted information," Bruno Ugg said.

"Want to go to the library now?" I asked.

"I want to get a Fudgsicle and cool out in the basement," Loretta Fischetti said. "I'm melting. Let's go see Starr Lackawanna tonight, when it's less hot."

We stopped at Sean Vergessen's store and arrived in the basement, Fudgsicles in hand, to find that someone had left part of a rusty sewing machine and half a tuna fish sandwich in the middle of the floor.

The plastic milk crate with the Classics Comics was gone.

We stood there, stunned. The Fudgsicles dripped.

"The phantom!" Bruno Ugg said. "We've been visited by the phantom!"

"Now it's personal," Loretta Fischetti said.

"It wasn't personal when my bike was stolen?" I asked.

"Now it's more personal," Loretta Fischetti said.

42

"As a scientist, I do not believe in phantoms," Starr Lackawanna said.

"You're a scientist?" I asked.

"Library science," Starr Lackawanna said. "I have a master's degree. Of course, I am very sorry that your Classics Comics were taken. We don't have any comics here at the library, but we have most of the original books they're based on. You are welcome to check them out."

"*Twenty Thousand Leagues Under the Sea*?" I asked.

"Certainly," Starr Lackawanna said. "Do you all want me to issue library cards to you?"

Starr Lackawanna typed our names on three official Hoboken Public Library cards. I had her type my name as Nick Nemo. I was pretty sure she knew that wasn't really my name—but she did it anyway

"So is Sibyl's Cave real, Ms. Lackawanna?" Loretta Fischetti asked.

"Not many people know about Sibyl's Cave," Starr Lackawanna said. "It's been sealed up since the eighteen eighties, and the entrance was covered up and concealed in nineteen thirty-seven. People were afraid that children would get lost in it."

"Like Tom Sawyer," I said. It was one of the best Classics Comics.

"Probably it was because of that book that people were concerned about children getting lost," Starr Lackawanna said. "We have that book, by the way, and I recommend it highly But you know, there wasn't really much danger of anyone getting lost in Sibyl's Cave. It's only about thirty feet long."

"Where is the cave exactly?" Bruno Ugg asked.

"You know Tesev Noskecnil Park?" Starr Lackawanna asked.

"We were there earlier today," Loretta Fischetti said.

"The cave is said to be under the park," Starr Lackawanna said. "It's quite a nice little park, with paths and stately trees, swings and slides for little children, a baseball field, and you must have noticed the handsome statue of Theodore Roosevelt, twenty-sixth President of the United States, between nineteen-oh-one and nineteen-oh-nine, and known as the Rough Rider, the Trust Buster, TR, and Teddy. Did you know the teddy bear was named in his honor?"

"What did you say he was called? The Trust Buster?" Loretta Fischetti asked.

"Yes," Starr Lackawanna said. "He busted the trusts—meaning he was against unfair practices by big companies and groups of companies that joined together as 'trusts' to suppress competition. Did you know he also helped to negotiate the end of a war between Russia and Japan at the beginning of the twentieth century?"

"So Buster is not the name of a person," Loretta Fischetti said.

"Not in this connection," Starr Lackawanna said. "Theodore Roosevelt visited this very library once. We have a photograph of him being issued a library card."

We checked out *The Adventures of Tom Sawyer* by Mark Twain, *Twenty Thousand Leagues Under the Sea* by Jules Verne, and *Treasure Island* by Robert Louis Stevenson, thanked Starr Lackawanna for all the information and the library cards, and went out into the muggy Hoboken night.

"So. Trust Buster," Loretta Fischetti said.

"Meehan the Bum said it was a clue," I said. "Let's take a good look at that statue in the park tomorrow."

43

I wound up taking *Treasure Island* home with me. I meant to just read the first few pages, but instead I read far into the night. When I slept, I was still with Jim Hawkins, Long John Silver, and the pirates on board the ship *Hispaniola.* When I woke up, I read some more. I had liked the Classics Comics version, but the real book was . . . well . . . real.

Even though I was walking and talking and being my normal self, part of me was still on the island with Jim Hawkins, Squire Trelawney, and Captain Smollett when I met with my friends. Bruno Ugg was deep into *Twenty Thousand Leagues Under the Sea*, and Loretta Fischetti was plowing through *The Adventures of Tom Sawyer*, We had agreed to inspect the Theodore Roosevelt statue in Tesev Noskecnil Park to see if we could figure out more about the "Trust Buster" clue, but under the circumstances, we decided to spend a couple of hours reading first.

Vic Trola's voice came over the radio, "That was 'I Gave You My Heart and a Diamond, and You Clubbed Me with a Spade,' by—" Someone reached out and clicked off the radio. I didn't look up to see who. We read on in silence.

44

We were in a sort of trance. Actually, three trances. When Loretta Fischetti's mother came down with turkey salad sandwiches, Cheez Doodles, and iced tea, it was as though we were suddenly awakened from sleep. We stretched and yawned and blinked. Then we realized we were wildly hungry.

The sandwiches disappeared first. The iced tea felt good going down, and the Cheez Doodles were crunchy and made our fingers and faces orangey yellow.

"What do you say, shall we go look over the Teddy Roosevelt statue now?" I asked.

"Yes, we should," Loretta Fischetti said. "If what Meehan the Bum said was true, if 'Trust Buster' is a clue to where the entrance to Sibyl's Cave is, then we have to plan to go there and try to get back our Classics Comics."

This was the first time any of us had actually said it.

"So we are going to try to get into the cave?" Bruno Ugg asked.

"I think we have to," Loretta Fischetti said. "It has our comics."

"And some of my father's comics. He's saved them since he was a boy," I said. "I don't want to have to tell him they're gone."

"But it's the phantom's cave now," Bruno Ugg said. "And we don't know anything about the phantom, how dangerous and evil it may be."

"I think we should be careful," Loretta Fischetti said. "But I think we have to try."

"We'll just have a look," I said. "It may not be a clue at all. Most of what Meehan said sounded like raving—most likely this is too."

"Well, if we're going, let's go," Bruno Ugg said.

We emerged into the heat wave. The citizens of Hoboken were sweating through their clothes—those who were in the street. Most people were probably indoors somewhere, sitting in front of air conditioners and fans. We made our way through the town, like a bunch of exhausted reptiles.

It was a little cooler under the trees in Tesev Noskecnil Park. At moments I imagined a little breeze was starting to happen—but it never did.

There was the statue of Teddy Roosevelt, big as life, and we had never noticed it before. TR was standing on a pedestal with sloping sides. His feet were a little higher than our heads. He was staring to the south and pointing to the southeast with his left hand. In his right hand he held a big stick.

"Wow! He looks sort of like a walrus," Bruno Ugg said.

"And look at those little goggles," I said.

"He looks determined," Loretta said.

"So where's the clue?" Bruno Ugg asked.

"This is like *Treasure Island*!" I said. "Look at his hand! He's pointing! Follow the finger!"

We crowded under the hand of the statue and tried to see where it was pointing. It was pointing to the baseball diamond.

"That's the clue? It's just ground!" Bruno Ugg said.

"What are we supposed to do, go at it with shovels?" Loretta Fischetti asked.

"I don't know. Maybe we're supposed to pry up home plate," I said.

"This is disappointing," Loretta Fischetti said.

"It's just like *Treasure Island*," I said. "Only it's a statue pointing instead of a skeleton pointing. But it's not pointing at anything in particular."

"That, or you don't know how to look," a voice said.

We turned around and saw someone sitting on a bench nearby. He had been listening to us talk. It was an old guy with long gray hair. He was wearing a Boston Red Sox jacket and silk slippers with red and gold dragons on them.

"What?" we said.

"You said the statue is not pointing at anything in particular," the old guy said. "I say you haven't explored all the possibilities."

"Such as what?" Loretta Fischetti asked the old guy.

"It's polite to introduce yourself when you converse with someone," the old guy said. "I am Sterling Mazzocchi, and to whom do I have the honor of speaking?"

We introduced ourselves. As each of us spoke our name, Sterling Mazzocchi bowed his head, and said, "Delighted."

"Such as what?" Loretta Fischetti asked again.

"Such as, has the statue always been in the place it now occupies? Has it always faced in the direction it now faces? How do you know it is pointing at the baseball diamond, when it might be pointing to something farther away?"

"But there's nothing visible beyond the baseball field but the Hudson River and New York City," I said.

"I just asked, 'how do you know?'" Sterling Mazzocchi said. "What if you carefully lined up a powerful telescope with the pointing finger and were able to read an inscription on the building in Manhattan it's indicating? Couldn't that be the clue you're looking for?"

"Do you know what clue we're looking for?" I asked.

"You're looking for the entrance to Sibyl's Cave, carefully hidden since nineteen thirty-seven," Sterling Mazzocchi said.

"Is there an inscription on a building in Manhattan telling us where to find it?" Loretta Fischetti asked.

"There could be," Sterling Mazzocchi said. "There's no reason why there couldn't be."

"Do you know there to be such an inscription?" I asked.

"No, I do not actually know for a fact—that is, I have not seen such an inscription myself, with my own eyes," Sterling Mazzocchi said.

"Do you believe there is such an inscription?" Bruno Ugg asked.

"No, I do not," Sterling Mazzocchi said.

"Do you know where the entrance to Sibyl's Cave is?" Loretta Fischetti asked.

"Yes. I know that," Sterling Mazzocchi said.

"Will you tell us?" I asked.

"No, I will not," Sterling Mazzocchi said.

"Why? Why will you not tell us?" Bruno asked.

"The entrance to the cave was concealed for the very reason that children might try to get into the cave, get lost, and die there," Sterling Mazzocchi said.

"But we were told the whole cave is only thirty feet long," I said.

"Yes, I believe that is so," Sterling Mazzocchi said.

"So we are not likely to be in very much danger," I said.

"Caves are dangerous," Sterling Mazzocchi said. "Anything can happen in a cave."

"Do you know about the phantom?" Loretta Fischetti asked Sterling Mazzocchi.

"Do you know what an urban legend is?" Sterling Mazzocchi asked Loretta Fischetti.

"Yes."

"The phantom is an urban legend," Sterling Mazzocchi said.

"The phantom stole Nick's bicycle and our joint collection of Classics Comics," Loretta Fischetti said. "Can a legend do that?"

"Some legends can, apparently," Sterling Mazzocchi said.

"Do you know about the giant chicken who once menaced Hoboken?" I asked.

"Yes, I do," Sterling Mazzocchi said.

"Is that a legend too?" I asked.

"No, the chicken is quite real," Sterling Mazzocchi said.

"Do you know where it is now?" I asked.

"I have been away for a long time. You should ask someone who knows a lot about Hoboken history and lore," Sterling Mazzocchi said. "Now if you will excuse me, I have to go take my rhumba lesson." So saying, the old man got up and walked out of Tesev Noskecnil Park.

"Odd fellow," I said.

"Not as insane as Meehan the Bum," Bruno Ugg said.

"His name is vaguely familiar," Loretta Fischetti said.

45

"Let's ask Starr Lackawanna if the Teddy Roosevelt statue was ever in a different location," Loretta Fischetti said. "If she doesn't know, she'll be able to look it up for us."

"When we asked her about the giant chicken, she dug up stuff about some other giant chicken that only weighs thirteen pounds," I said.

"But she's friendly and wants to help," Loretta Fischetti said. "She would have dug up more about the chicken if we had asked her—and she came through with information about the cave and accidentally explained 'Trust Buster.'"

"She gave us library cards and checked out great books to us," Bruno Ugg said. "And she is the only adult who seems to want to talk to us who isn't a crazy old man in the park."

"Okay I agree," I said. "Starr Lackawanna is cool. Let's go talk to her."

As we came through the door of the library Starr Lackawanna said, "Oh, children! I found more giant chicken information for you!"

Loretta Fischetti looked at us triumphantly. "What did I tell you?" she said.

"Did you know that a giant chicken, more than six feet tall, once rampaged through the streets of Hoboken?" Starr Lackawanna asked.

"Yes, we knew that," we said.

"Did you know her name was Henrietta, and she was the pet of a little boy named Arthur Bobowicz?" Starr Lackawanna asked.

"Yes, we knew that," we said.

"Did you know that the chicken went wild for a while and the citizens panicked?" Starr Lackawanna asked.

"Yes, we knew that," we said.

"And that the chicken finally calmed down and was reunited with little Arthur?" Starr Lackawanna asked.

"Yes, we knew that," we said.

"And that the chicken was bred right here in Hoboken by a mad scientist named Professor Mazzocchi?"

"We knew that, but we forgot," we said. "Did you say Mazzocchi? What was his first name?"

"Sterling," Starr Lackawanna said. "It was Sterling. I never forget a first name."

"Astonishing!" I said.

"Amazing!" Bruno Ugg said.

"Astounding!" Loretta Fischetti said.

"I live to astonish, amaze, and astound," Starr Lackawanna said. "Those are things librarians do well."

"Did you find all this out from old newspaper articles?" Loretta Fischetti asked.

"Yes, I did," Starr Lackawanna said.

"Do you know where Henrietta the giant chicken is today?" I asked Starr Lackawanna.

"No. Do you want me to keep looking up facts?" the librarian asked.

"We are interested in Henrietta the giant chicken," Loretta Fischetti said. "But there's something we're more urgently interested in. We need to know if the Teddy Roosevelt statue in the park ever stood in a different location. Do you happen to remember?"

"I only moved to Hoboken six months ago, so I wouldn't remember personally," Starr Lackawanna said. "But we can do some checking. Come down to the basement where the maps and plans are kept."

As we followed Starr Lackawanna down the steps to the map room in the library basement, Loretta Fischetti whispered to Bruno Ugg and me, "I thought I recognized that name. The guy in the park was Professor Mazzocchi!"

"Do you think it's the same guy?" I whispered to Loretta Fischetti.

"Unless there are two people named Sterling Mazzocchi who know about the chicken," Loretta Fischetti said.

"Then it's him! We have to find him again!" I said.

"We have the phantom to deal with first," Loretta Fischetti said. "The giant chicken can wait."

46

"Here's a piece of luck!" Starr Lackawanna said as she unrolled a big dusty piece of paper. "It's an aerial photograph, taken from a dirigible, probably, in nineteen thirty-nine. It shows Tesev Noskecnil Park, which was then known as Evest Linkecsno Park."

"What's a dirigible?" Bruno Ugg asked Loretta Fischetti.

"Blimp," Loretta Fischetti said.

"Hey!" Bruno Ugg said.

"Yes, it's the park all right," Starr Lackawanna said. "And here is the statue—and look! It is facing Manhattan! It was turned at some point, just as you children suspected!"

"What is that building the statue's hand is pointing to?" I asked Starr Lackawanna.

"That would be the Hoboken Academy of Art," Starr Lackawanna said. "I read up on it. It is a fine building in the Beaux-Arts style. It was built in eighteen eighty-three and was first known as the Hoboken Academy of Beaux-Arts."

"It's an art school? Hoboken has an art school?" I asked.

"It was one. It stopped being an art school in nineteen thirty-nine. It specialized in avant-garde—that's ultra-modern—art. They had classes in Impossibleism, Supersurrealism, Dynamic Double-Daddy Realism, Ishkabibbleism, and Mama."

"Mama?"

"Like Dada, only nicer," Starr Lackawanna said. "After the art school closed, the building was used for offices, apartments, and a live poultry market. I think it's just offices now. By the way, how are you kids doing with the books you checked out? Ready for more?"

"We're going to swap around before we turn them back in," Bruno Ugg said.

"That's fine. Just remember, I have plenty of other books, and you're entitled to check them all out," Starr Lackawanna said. "Did you get what you wanted about the statue?"

"Yes, thanks," Loretta Fischetti said.

"Any time you need help, that's what I'm here for," Starr Lackawanna said.

47

C—that's the way it begins.
H—I'm the second one in.
I—I am the third, and
C—I'm the fourth letter of that bird, oh,
K—I'm movin' in.
E—I'm near the n.
Oh, c-h-i-c-k-e-n,
That's the way you spell chicken

"Look! It's Vic Trola!" Bruno Ugg said.

Vic Trola was sitting at a table in the Mercury Lunchroom. He was eating a bowl of oyster stew and reading a comic book.

"Let's go in and talk to him," I said. "He knows all about Hoboken history and odd facts. We never asked him if he knew anything about Henrietta the giant chicken."

"What is it with you and that chicken?" Loretta Fischetti asked.

"I want to know, that's all," I said.

"We're supposed to be tracking down the entrance to Sibyl's Cave—and you'll remember that Vic Trola went all panicky when we asked if he knew anything about the phantom," Loretta Fischetti said. "He may be the biggest nutcase we've run into so far—and who eats oyster stew when it's one hundred degrees in the shade? In fact, who eats oyster stew at any time?"

"We'll be indirect," I said. "We'll just stop in and chat for a few minutes. Maybe he'll tell us something without meaning to."

"Say! That looks like a Classics Comic he's reading," Bruno Ugg said.

"Now I'm interested," Loretta Fischetti said. "Just act natural—like we're fans of the radio show. I'd like to know where he got that comic."

We sauntered into the Mercury Lunchroom and pretended not to notice Vic Trola at first.

"Boy, is it hot!" I said.

"I sure feel like a lemonade," Bruno Ugg said.

"Hey! It's Vic Trola!" Loretta Fischetti said. "Hi, Mr. Trola!"

"Oh, hi, kids," Vic Trola said, looking up from his disgusting oyster stew and his comic book. "You can call me Vic."

"Vic, we have certainly been enjoying the songs you play on the radio," I said.

"Yes, we certainly have," Loretta Fischetti said.

"'*C-h-i-c-k-e-n,*'" Bruno Ugg sang, "'that's the way to spell *chicken.*'"

"Don't push it," Loretta whispered to Bruno.

Vic Trola smiled a big smile. "I have old records nobody has," he said. "Come and sit with me."

We crowded into the booth.

"Yeah, I love those records you play," Bruno Ugg said. "I guess you have a big collection."

"I have thousands," Vic Trola said. "May I buy you all a soda or a lemonade—or does anyone want a taste of my oyster stew?"

"Yich! I mean, we'll just have cold drinks, thanks," Loretta Fischetti said. "Our mothers don't want us to eat between meals."

"What comic is that?" I asked.

"It's a Classics Comic," Vic Trola said. "*Kim* by Rudyard Kipling."

"That's old, isn't it?" I asked.

"Yes, I think so," Vic Trola said.

"I don't think they sell Classics Comics anymore," I said.

"That so?" Vic Trola said. "It's a pretty good comic."

The waitress brought us glasses of lemonade.

"Thanks for the lemonades, Vic," Loretta Fischetti said.

"It's a pleasure to treat my young fans," Vic Trola said. "Not many kids like my radio station. Mostly I get older people who remember the songs."

"Well, we don't listen to any other station," I said. "So where did you get the comic?"

I could sense that Bruno Ugg and Loretta Fischetti were a little tense when I asked a direct question. I knew they were afraid that Vic Trola would freak out—but he didn't.

"My mommy," he said.

"Your mommy?"

"Yes, my mommy lives upstairs. She left it lying around. Good comic," Vic Trola said. "Usually I read action comics, like *The Silver Avenger* and *Captain Justice*. By the way, be sure to tune in tomorrow. I found some Memphis Minnie records in a garage sale—I'm going to play some of them on the air."

"So your mommy likes comics?" I asked.

"She just happened to have this one," Vic Trola said. He looked at his watch. "I have to get back to the station pretty soon. The tape I have playing will end in twelve minutes. Vic Trola slurped up the last of his nauseating oyster stew, left a tip for the waitress, and paid the tab at the cash register. "Keep listening to Radio Jolly Roger, okay?" He took a toothpick from the little toothpick dispenser, put it in his mouth, and strolled out of the Mercury Lunchroom.

"We will!" we called after him. "Thanks again for the lemonades!"

"Well, that was normal," Bruno Ugg said.

"It was," Loretta Fischetti said. "Except that he had a Classics Comic, and ours are missing."

"It doesn't prove anything,"I said. "He said he got it from his mommy. I got mine from my daddy—I mean my father. He didn't act guilty or nervous."

"Still, it's quite a coincidence, you have to admit," Loretta Fischetti said.

"The chicken song is a coincidence too," Bruno Ugg said.

"It is that," I said. "But Vic Trola doesn't seem evil or nasty or anything. He's just a harmless, music-loving, oyster stew-eating freak who lives with his mommy."

"I'd like to know where his mommy got that comic," Loretta Fischetti said. "Do you suppose it's one of ours, and someone is selling them on the streets of Hoboken?"

"I hadn't thought of that," Bruno Ugg said.

"Neither had I," I said.

48

The former Hoboken Academy of Art was across the street from Tesev Noskecnil Park.

"It's quite a fancy building," I said. "It's funny we never noticed it before."

I guess that's the Beaux-Arts style of architecture," Bruno Ugg said. "Look at all the ornaments and doodads and wiggly things on it."

"Sort of a cross between a wedding cake and a nightmare," Loretta Fischetti said. "I like it."

"I like it too," I said. "Somebody ought to wash it."

"Let's go in and look around," Loretta Fischetti said.

We went up the wide steps and through the big front door. Inside there was an open space with a high ceiling and more Beaux-Arts stuff all over everything. There were statues built into the walls. Everything was marble, and it was as grimy and crummy as the outside. A few more steps led up to a big open lobby. There was a staircase going up, and hallways leading off to the sides. We could hear voices coming from behind closed doors, the sound of a typewriter or computer printer, and the sound of shoes walking on the marble floor—but we didn't see anyone.

"So where do you suppose the secret entrance to the cave is?" I asked.

We wandered around the lobby, looking. At the back of the lobby, underneath the staircase, was the only thing in

the place that wasn't Beaux-Arts looking. It was a big
metal door with flaking black paint on it. There was a
paper sign glued to the door:

NO ADMITTANCE!
Sealed by order of Matthias Krumwald,
Commissioner of Public Works, City of
Hoboken, November 17, 1937.

"And this would be the secret entrance," Loretta
Fischetti said.

"This? Some secret," I said.

"Well, nineteen thirty-seven," Loretta Fischetti said.
"That's when they sealed up the cave so kids wouldn't
wander in, get lost, and die."

"How do you get lost in a cave that's only thirty feet?" I
asked.

"Maybe that's only the story that people believe,"
Bruno Ugg said. "You know, an urban myth. Maybe they
sealed it up so people couldn't use the cave to make illegal fermented sauerkraut."

"Right," I said. "Meehan the Bum mentioned that. So if
it's sealed, how can we get in?"

"Let's see how sealed it really is," Loretta Fischetti
said.

There wasn't any handle on the door and no lock. It
appeared to be attached to the marble wall with big
screws. We got our fingernails around the edge and
tugged. It wiggled a little. We all grabbed the edge on one
side and pulled. It wiggled, but it didn't move. Then we
tried prying the other side with our fingers. The door
opened a tiny bit. We got a better grip and pulled again. It
swung open a few inches.

"Easy as pie," I said.

We pulled the door open enough for me to stick my
head inside. I could just make out the beginning of a flight
of stairs going down.

"Stairs! Carved out of the living rock," I said. "It's pretty dark, though."

"We need flashlights," Bruno Ugg said. "Shall we go get some and go exploring?"

"I think we have to," Loretta Fischetti said.

"Wait!" Bruno Ugg said. "What if the phantom is down there? What if it lives down there?"

"Good point," I said. We pushed the door closed and took a few steps back.

"You saw the phantom that time, at the Bat Hat Festival," Loretta Fischetti said. "Did it look dangerous?"

"It was tall," I said. "I just had a glimpse. I can't say whether it looked dangerous or not. I don't think I want to meet it in a cave."

"I think we should come back at night," Loretta Fischetti said.

"At night?"

"At night is when the phantom prowls the streets of Hoboken, taking people's comic books and leaving them junk and tuna fish sandwiches."

"But at night it's dark," Bruno Ugg said.

"It's a cave," Loretta Fischetti said. "It's always dark."

49

"What's on the schedule for this evening, old graham cracker?" my father asked. He pronounced *schedule* "shed-yule."

"I'm going to explore a cave with my friends," I said. "That's why I'm borrowing the flashlight."

"Ah, the fascinating sport of spelunking, eh? Jolly good fun," my father said. "Be very careful not to fall into a pit and break all your bones, or drown in an underground pool, or get lost and starve and go mad in the darkness. Ah, youth! I wish I were going with you! But I have to stay here and strip wallpaper, dash the luck."

"Thanks for the loan of the flashlight," I told my father. I still hadn't told him that his Classics Comics were among the missing. With good luck, I'd get them back, and he'd never have to know.

"Going out, Ivan?" my mother asked.

"Going spelunking, Mother," I said.

"Take a sweater! It gets cold in caves," my mother said.

50

"What if someone locked the front door?" Bruno Ugg asked.

"I never thought of that," Loretta Fischetti said. "If we were to bust in, we'd be breaking the law."

"We're going to bust into the cave," Bruno Ugg said.

"Not really," Loretta Fischetti said. "The door to the cave isn't really locked."

"Yes, but the sign says 'No Admittance,'" Bruno Ugg said.

"'No Admittance,' in 1937," Loretta Fischetti said. "Don't official things expire after twenty-five years or something?"

"Let's just try the door," I said. We walked up the stairs and pulled the handle. The door swung open.

"Look at that. It wasn't locked," Bruno Ugg said.

"Look at that," Loretta Fischetti said.

"Yeah, look at that," I said.

We stood there in the doorway, about to enter the Hoboken Academy of Art, at night, with the intention of opening the door, officially sealed in 1937, that led to Sibyl's Cave. What if a cop came by? Would we be arrested for burglary and spelunking without a license?

A cop came by.

"Good evening, kids," the cop said. It was Officer Spooney. "Not up to any mischief, I hope."

"No, sir," we said.

"Well, don't stay out too late and worry your parents," Officer Spooney said. He continued along the street, whistling.

"Let's get inside," Loretta Fischetti said. "Everybody got your flashlight? Everybody got a hat?"

51

The lobby of the Hoboken Academy of Art was dimly lit by a couple of dinky lightbulbs. We made our way to the metal door under the stairs, pulled it open, and pointed our flashlights down the steps. The steps went down and down. Our flashlights made three white pencils of light. They hardly made a dent in the blackness.

"Let's go," Loretta Fischetti said.

We started down. I would have thought it would be cool, like our basements, going down stairs into a cave, but the air that rose from the deep below was hot and had a sour smell.

My knees were shaking. I thought the other kids were scared, too, but no one said anything, and we kept going down, a step at a time.

"What if there are bats?" Bruno Ugg said.

"Then we'll finally get to see one," Loretta Fischetti said.

"Are you sure this is a good idea?" I asked.

"You want to go back?" Loretta Fischetti asked.

I wanted to say yes, but instead I heard myself saying, "No. Of course not."

"Right," Loretta Fischetti said. "Our Classics Comics might be down here."

"And my bicycle might be down here," I said.

"What . . . is . . . that smell?" Bruno Ugg said.

"It smells like . . .What . . . does . . . it smell like?" Loretta Fischetti said.

"It smells sort of like—," I began.

"Sauerkraut!" Bruno Ugg said. "It smells like sauer-kraut!"

"Illegal fermented sauerkraut that they used to make in the cave?" I asked.

"Sauerkraut from more than sixty years ago? And we can still smell it?" Loretta Fischetti asked.

"That's some sauerkraut," I said.

The smell was a lot stronger as we got to the bottom of the steps.

"It's the cave! We're in the cave!" Bruno Ugg said.

It was the cave all right. It looked like . . . a cave. It had a high, rounded ceiling, and everything was rough and rocky. It was mostly totally, incredibly, completely dark—blacker than the blackest night. The sauerkraut smell was intense. It was making my eyes water. It was making my head spin. The flashlight beams picked up some glints of metal and flashes of color.

"Look! Bicycles!" Loretta Fischetti said. Her voice sounded raspy The sauerkraut fumes were making her choke.

"So it's true!" Bruno Ugg gasped. "This is where the phantom hides stuff."

"Where are the comics?" Loretta Fischetti said as she sank to the cave floor. Then she said, "The sauerkraut. I can't . . ."

My knees were giving way. I'm not sure I said the words or just thought them as I lost consciousness. "This is funny We're being suffocated by ancient sauerkraut fumes. We kids are going to die down here, just like every-one said."

Then I thought, Uh-oh. I'm dead.

52

So there I was, dead. Lying dead with my two friends, Loretta Fischetti and Bruno Ugg. Being dead wasn't too bad—a little boring. We just lay there. Dead. Dead as could be. Lying there. On the grass. Dead. Dead on the grass on the floor of Sibyl's Cave. Dead on the grass? On what grass? I wiggled my dead fingers and felt. It was grass, all right. There's no grass in caves. Was I in heaven already?

I had closed my eyes. It seemed like the right thing to do, being dead and all. I opened one eye and saw a white light. I had heard about this. When you die, you see a white light. Then angels come and explain to you that you're dead, and after a while God comes around and gives you a letter grade for what kind of person you had been. The lowest grade I ever got in school was B-, but it was possible that points would be deducted for going into a cave that had been sealed by the Commissioner of Public Works.

There were moths flying around the white light. I opened the other eye. It looked a lot like a streetlight, the kind they have in Tesev Noskecnil Park.

"We're in the park," Loretta Fischetti said.

"We are?" I asked.

"I think we are," Bruno Ugg said.

We sat up. We were in the park, on the grass. I could still smell the sauerkraut a little, and there was another smell—I thought it was sort of chickeny. Beside us was the plastic milk crate with our Classics Comics in it!

"Wow! I thought I was dead," I said.

"Me too," Bruno Ugg said.

"I saw you hit the floor," I told Loretta Fischetti. "Did you get Bruno and me out of the cave and rescue the comics, and if so, how did you do it?"

"I didn't do anything that I know of," Loretta Fischetti said. "I don't know how we got here."

"I think the giant chicken saved us," I said. I didn't know why I said that, except that was what I thought.

"Well, I can't say you're wrong," Loretta Fischetti said. "Because I don't know what actually happened, but I can say that you have that giant chicken on the brain." She brushed a white feather off her shoulder.

"It was the giant chicken," I said. "It saved us."

53

We took turns carrying the milk crate full of Classics Comics. When we got to our buildings, my father and Loretta Fischetti's father, Lance Fischetti, were sitting on the steps, smoking cigars.

"Hi, kids," Mr. Fischetti said. "How did the spelunking go?"

"We got killed," Bruno Ugg said. "But we're all right now."

"Nick thinks we were rescued by the giant chicken," Loretta Fischetti said.

"Ah, childhood!" my father said. "It's a magical fairyland of imaginary adventures."

"It's almost your bedtime, miss," Mr. Fischetti said to his daughter. "You'd better get upstairs—and you too, young Bruno Ugg."

"Be careful when you take your shower, old Fig Newton," my father told me. "Your mother and I pulled up the floor in the bathroom. Walk on the beams."

"It really was the giant chicken that saved us," I said.

"It's great, the things kids come up with," Lance Fischetti said.

"We'll see you in the morning," Loretta Fischetti and Bruno Ugg told me.

54

In the morning the first thing we did was check our Classics Comics. Bruno Ugg had listed them all by title and number in a notebook, and we compared the comics in the milk crate to the list. They were all there—except one.

"It seems the only comic missing is number one-forty-three," Loretta Fischetti said.

"And number one-forty-three is?" I asked.

"*Kim*, by Rudyard Kipling," Loretta Fischetti said.

"The comic Vic Trola was reading in the Mercury Lunchroom!" Bruno Ugg said.

We were silent for a while.

"Vic Trola is tall," I said.

"Vic Trola got all nervous the time we asked him if he knew anything about the phantom," Bruno Ugg said.

"Vic Trola said he got the comic from his mommy," Loretta Fischetti said.

"Which he did not," I said.

"He was reading our comic!" Bruno Ugg said.

"Which he stole from us!" Loretta Fischetti said.

"And left us a piece of broken junk and half a tuna fish sandwich!" I said.

"Which means . . ."

"Vic Trola is the phantom!" we all said at once.

"And he has my bicycle!" I said.

"He's a skunk!" Bruno Ugg said.

"Although, he probably saved our lives. It must have been Vic Trola who dragged us out of the cave when we were overcome with fermented sauerkraut fumes," Loretta Fischetti said.

"No, that was the giant chicken," I said.

"You're so sure about that. How do you know it was the giant chicken?" Loretta Fischetti asked me.

"I just know," I said. "I don't know how I know, but I do."

"What are we going to do about Vic Trola?" Bruno Ugg asked.

"Make him give back my bicycle," I said.

"There were a number of bicycles in the cave," Loretta Fischetti said. "Officer Spooney mentioned that there had been other thefts. We should make Vic Trola give back all the bicycles."

"We're not afraid of Vic Trola, right?" Bruno Ugg asked.

"I'm certainly not afraid of him," Loretta Fischetti said. "I might give him a knuckle sandwich—except he did probably save our lives."

"I'm pretty sure that was the chicken," I said.

"We know," Loretta Fischetti said. "The point is that Vic Trola isn't scary."

"I was sort of scared of the phantom when I didn't know who it was," I said. "But Vic Trola is more pathetic than frightening."

"That's true," Bruno Ugg said. "Being a phantom must be some kind of mental disorder. Let's threaten him first, and then suggest he seek medical help."

"We going to threaten him now?" I asked.

"There's no time like the present," Loretta Fischetti said.

55

"Maybe we should take some adult muscle with us," I said. "I mean, he is a criminal."

"The cops?" Bruno Ugg said.

"No, not the cops," Loretta Fischetti said. "They would sort of take over—and I want to confront Vic Trola myself. But I do agree, it might be a good idea to have a grown-up or two just in case he goes nuts or something."

Just then my father appeared at the head of the basement stairs. "I say, old top, are you down there? I just want your opinion—your mother and I have found this perfectly spiffing stuffed Indian fruit bat, and we wondered if you'd like it for your room." He was brandishing a very large stuffed bat with neat glass eyes. It *was* sort of spiffing, I had to admit.

"You appear at just the right moment," I told my father. "We are just going to confront the guy who stole my bicycle and were wondering if you'd like to come along and help confront."

"It sounds jolly" my father said. "You won't mind if your mother comes along too? She enjoys a confrontation as much as I do."

"That will be fine," Loretta Fischetti said.

"Topping!" my father said. "I'll just call the memsaab—and I'll bring along the fruit bat, just in case the blighter needs any persuading." He bounded off to get my mother.

"Do you understand what he says?" Bruno Ugg asked me.

"Mostly," I said.

As Loretta Fischetti, Bruno Ugg, my mother and father, and I made our way through the streets to the building where Gugliermo Marconi had once lived, I explained things to my father. "He stole our Classics Comics, but we have them all back—all but one."

"What? He took my Classics Comics as well?" my father asked. "The bounder! If he offers resistance, I shall give him a bunch of fives, mark my words."

"This could never have happened in the suburbs," my mother said happily

56

We could see Vic Trola through the picture window. He was in his living room studio, with his earphones on, broadcasting.

We all crowded in without knocking.

"Hey! It's my fans!" Vic Trola said.

"We have the goods on you, buster," Loretta Fischetti said.

"Keep your hands where we can see them, sirrah!" my father said. "This is a stuffed Indian fruit bat, and I know how to use it."

Vic Trola said things like, "Wha? Huh? Wha?"

"We know about my stolen bicycle," I said. "And the other bicycles. We know you're the phantom, and we know where you got that comic book."

"Okay, okay. Ill talk," Vic Trola said. "Just let me get off the air—and keep that fruit bat away from me."

"Make it snappy sparky," Bruno Ugg said. "We're not playing here."

"Radio Jolly Roger now leaves the air . . . for transmitter repairs," Vic Trola said. "This is WRJR in beautiful Hoboken, New Jersey, signing off." He threw a switch and the red and green lights on the console went out. I had to admire how professional he was, even at the moment of getting busted for being the phantom.

"It wasn't me," Vic Trola said.

"Yeah, right," Loretta Fischetti said. "Who was it then, your mommy who lives upstairs?"

"I bet you don't even have a mommy living upstairs," Bruno Ugg said.

"No, my mommy lives in Florida under an assumed name. I just say it's my mommy living upstairs so people won't get curious."

"You, sir, are a rotter!" my father said. "I have a good mind to call the rozzers and have them clap the darbys on you."

"I don't know what that means," Vic Trola said. "But I ask you to allow me to tell my story."

"Very well," my father said. "But what you say had better be the emmis, or well give you to the peelers."

"Please be seated," Vic Trola said. "And help yourselves to dried apricots. My story is a strange and a sad one—but, speaking of strange, who is that woman tapping on the window?"

It was Starr Lackawanna. We motioned for her to come in.

"I was just out jogging, and I saw you all in here," Starr Lackawanna said. "I hope I am not interrupting."

"This man is Vic Trola. He is about to confess," I said. "These are my parents. Parents, this is Starr Lackawanna, the librarian."

"Ivan speaks highly of you," my mother said.

Starr Lackawanna flipped open a spiral notebook. "I will take down his confession," she said. "It's always best to make a record of such things. You may commence confessing."

"My real name," Vic Trola began, "is Arthur Bobowicz."

"Wow!" I said.

"Wow!" Bruno Ugg said.

"Wow!" Loretta Fischetti said.

"Wow!" Starr Lackawanna said, writing it down.

"Wow?" my mother and father asked.

"Years ago, when I was no older than these children, I acquired a pet from a mad scientist. It was, as most of you seem to know already, a giant chicken. I named her Henrietta. Henrietta was a good chicken, and I came to love her, but one day she ran amok."

"Amok," Starr Lackawanna said, writing it down.

"People were not used to seeing a giant chicken, six feet tall, running in the streets. I take it you all know the story of the general panic that ensued."

We nodded. We all knew.

"Once things had calmed down and Henrietta had come home, my life was normal. I was just an ordinary boy, with a pet giant chicken. I grew up. I attended the Columbia School of Pirate Broadcasting. In time, I realized my life's dream and opened a pirate radio station, right here in this house, once the residence of Gugliermo Marconi.

"My chicken remained with me through the years. Often in the evening, we would take walks in the park and swing on the swings and slide on the slides in the children's playground, as we had done since I was a child. I was happy in my work, broadcasting songs to the citizens of Hoboken."

"I like to swing on swings and slide on slides," Starr Lackawanna said. "Did you ever go on dates?"

"It's difficult to find women who want to go on dates that include a giant chicken," Vic Trola/Arthur Bobowicz said.

Starr Lackawanna made a note in the margin. "Continue," she said.

"My life was simple but satisfying. And then I became aware that Henrietta was going out by herself at night. At first I thought nothing of it. Then I discovered that she was making tuna fish sandwiches. I could tell because she is rather messy in the kitchen, being a chicken. It seemed strange because she herself hates tuna fish. Why was she making the sandwiches, and what was she doing with them?

"Like so many others, I heard stories of a phantom, a mysterious creature that took things, and left broken machinery . . . and tuna fish sandwiches in their place. I didn't make a connection at first. Then I began to suspect—but I refused to believe it could be *my* chicken. I knew she was a good chicken—she could never take bicycles that did not belong to her—it had to be a strange coincidence.

"But then she began to bring things home, especially the bells off bicycles. I would hear her ringing them in the night. On some level I knew she was the phantom, but still I refused to admit it to myself. I remembered the public outrage when she had run amok—but then she didn't actually do anything wrong; she just rampaged a bit. I didn't want to think of the consequences if she were stealing things.

"When you children came here and asked me what I knew about the phantom, I panicked. I knew events were closing in, and soon she would be discovered. I knew I would have to do something. I had almost made up my mind to go to the police—and then you all came here and confronted."

"Where is the chicken now?" I asked.

"She is upstairs, in her room," Arthur Bobowicz said. "I heard her ringing a bicycle bell a little while ago."

"Could you go and get her?" I asked.

"Certainly," Arthur Bobowicz said. "I will bring her right down—but first, I would like to say, I am glad you confronted. I feel sad, but strangely relieved."

Arthur Bobowicz left the living-room studio.

"I don't think he is a bad man," Starr Lackawanna said. "Just profoundly odd."

"Growing up with a giant chicken as a pet might do that to a person," my mother said.

"He is more to be pitied than censured," my father said.

57

Arthur Bobowicz returned with Henrietta. She was wonderful. I had never seen a chicken I liked so much, let alone one that was six feet tall. There was something tender and sad in her beautiful red eyes. I felt a great warmth coming from her.

"Ohhh, she's lovely," my mother said.

"Gee," Bruno Ugg said.

"Gosh," Loretta Fischetti said.

"Who's a pretty bird?" my father said.

"CLUCK!" Henrietta said.

"We all admire Henrietta," Starr Lackawanna said.

"She is a good bird," Arthur Bobowicz said. "But why has she turned into a phantom, and why is she doing bad things?"

"I believe I can answer that," a voice said. Someone else was in the room.

We turned and saw a man with long gray hair, wearing a Boston Red Sox jacket and silk slippers with red and gold dragons on them.

Professor Mazzocchi!" Arthur Bobowicz said.

"Yes, Arthur, it is I. I am happy to see you all grown up into a profoundly odd adult. And what a fine bird Number Seventy-three has become! She is one of my finest super-chickens, and I am proud of her."

"She's gone bad, Professor," Arthur Bobowicz said. "She's become a phantom, and she steals things."

"Yes, yes, I know all about it. That is the reason I have come back to Hoboken. I am here to help you. And Henrietta does not realize she is stealing. She is merely exchanging. She means no harm."

By this time I was standing right next to Henrietta. I hugged her. "I am sure she means no harm," I said.

"You know all about it?" Arthur Bobowicz asked.

"Indeed I do," Sterling Mazzocchi said. "When one is a mad scientist, so many of one's experiments go wrong, turn out evil, try to destroy the planet—it happens again and again. One learns to deal with it."

"How does one deal with it?" I asked.

"Well, usually I leave town," Sterling Mazzocchi said. "But I like to help when I can."

"And in this case?" Arthur Bobowicz asked.

"I can," Sterling Mazzocchi said. "An experimental giant chicken is sort of a blank slate. You don't know what to expect because it's never existed before. I bred my super-chickens not only for size but for personality and sweet-ness of temperament. And, as you can see, Henrietta is a charming sort of chicken."

"She certainly is," I said, stroking her soft feathers.

"But, I have noticed," Sterling Mazzocchi continued, "that about twenty years on, my chickens tend to exhibit some little oddities. Phantomic behavior is common. So I came to Hoboken, to see how Number Seventy-three was getting along and to offer some help if I could."

"Deuced marvelous. The man's a wonder!" my father said.

"So you can help her?" Arthur Bobowicz asked.

"It's not as simple as just giving her an injection of Mazzocchi's all-purpose curative Number Fourteen, or fitting her with a Mazzocchi Thought-Correcting Helmet," the professor said. "I tried those things on some of the others. What will help Henrietta is a change in the way she's treated."

"What do I have to do?" Arthur Bobowicz asked.

"Well, you see, Arthur, it's not something you, person-ally, can do. Henrietta is your chicken, and she loves you, but . . . well, you are all grown up and busy with your fine pirate radio station and . . . well, to put it as delicately as I can, you can't communicate with her the way you did when you were a boy."

"I can't?" Arthur Bobowicz asked.

"Oh, it's not that you have neglected her, and even if you were to spend a great deal more time with her, she might still do wild things. It's like this—in some Asian countries water buffalo are used in much the way we would use a tractor. Those beasts are no different from the wild ver-sion of the same animal—an ugly customer, bad tempered, strong, and unpredictable. Do you know how they tame them, and who looks after them? Boys! Little boys! They send out these little fellows on the backs of great big buffalo with huge horns, and the buffalo are as docile as moo-cows. It's often been observed that children and youngsters can control horses no adult can come near.

"Just look at Henrietta now, and your young friend . . . what is the name? Nick? See how calm and affectionate she is? She's content. She trusts him, and he trusts her. She won't be going out to trade tuna fish sandwiches for bicycles this night, I promise you."

"So what you're saying we have to do is?" Arthur Bobowicz asked.

"I am saying, Nick here is a fine boy. Nick, you are a boy who trusts a chicken, and I like that. Would you be willing to spend some time with this chicken every day or so? Take her around with you, play with her, just allow her to keep you company while you study or read?"

"Sure," I said. "There is nothing I'd like better."

"Henrietta is welcome at the Hoboken Public Library," Starr Lackawanna said.

"And Henrietta can hang out in our basement where we like to read, and listen to Vic Trola . . . uh, Arthur Bobowicz, on the radio," Loretta Fischetti said.

"Well, if that is so, then the chicken will soon be rehabilitated," Sterling Mazzocchi said. "All it takes is a bit of kindness."

"Oh, this is such an urban thing to have happen!" my mother said. "A giant chicken! This is the kind of rich life experience your father and I wanted you to have."

My father patted me on the shoulder. "Jolly good show, old man," he said.

58

"All that remains is to get those bicycles out of the cave," I said.

"Only there are lethal fermented sauerkraut fumes down there," Loretta Fischetti said. "Which apparently have no effect on giant chickens—yes, Nick, I agree it was Henrietta who saved us—but humans can't go down there."

"I can help you," Professor Mazzocchi said. "I happen to have my Mazzocchi Featherweight Diving Helmet in my station wagon. I will be happy to bring the bicycles out."

We trooped across Tesev Noskecnil Park, Professor Mazzocchi carrying his diving helmet. Then eight of us, seven humans and the chicken, stood around in the lobby of the Hoboken Academy of Art while Sterling Mazzocchi handed up the bicycles, one by one. Mine was there, and nine others, all shapes and sizes. We wheeled them through the lobby and lined them up on the sidewalk.

"What now?" I asked. "Do we call the police?"

"No, let's take a ride," my father said. "Three times around the park and then we'll deliver them to the constabulary in person. Everyone agree?"

"There are nine of us, including Henrietta," Starr Lackawanna said. "Can the chicken ride a bike?"

"She stole them. What do you think?" Arthur Bobowicz asked.

211

"Oh, Arthur, you're so droll," Starr Lackawanna said. "But we're still a rider short."

"I think I see Meehan the Bum," I said. "Hey, Mr. Meehan, can you ride a bike?"

"I finished fourth in the Tour de France," Meehan shouted back.

So we all mounted our bikes. We must have made a strange picture, kids, normal grown-ups, the not-so-normal Meehan and Professor Mazzocchi, on bikes of all sizes, and a giant chicken riding one of those adult tricycles. We pedaled slowly, making a big, graceful circle around the park, laughing and talking. Then we made another. As we began the third time around, the leaves began to tremble above us, and a cool breeze blew in from New York Harbor.